For those who savor the unusual, here are twelve
tales of another world, where anything is possible
for nothing is quite as it seems:

ALSO BY

JACK FINNEY

The House of Numbers

The Third Level

by JACK FINNEY

A Dell Book

Published by
DELL PUBLISHING CO., INC.
750 Third Avenue
New York 17, N.Y.

© Copyright, 1949, 1950, 1951, 1952, 1955,
1956, 1957, by Jack Finney

© Copyright, 1948, by The Curtis Publishing Company

Reprinted by arrangement with
Rinehart & Company, Inc.
New York, N.Y.

Designed and produced by
Western Printing & Lithographing Company

First Dell printing—March, 1959

Printed in U.S.A.

The presidents of the New York Central and the New York, New Haven and Hartford railroads will swear on a stack of timetables that there are only two. But I say there are three, because I've *been* on the third level at Grand Central Station. Yes, I've taken the obvious step: I talked to a psychiatrist friend of mine, among others. I told him about the third level at Grand Central Station, and he said it was a waking-dream wish fulfillment. He said I was unhappy. That made my wife kind of mad, but he explained that he meant the modern world is full of insecurity, fear, war, worry and all the rest of it, and that I just want to escape. Well, hell, who doesn't? Everybody I know wants to escape, but they don't wander down into any third level at Grand Central Station.

But that's the reason, he said, and my friends all agreed. Everything points to it, they claimed. My stamp collecting, for example; that's a "temporary refuge from reality." Well, maybe, but my grandfather didn't need any refuge from reality; things were pretty nice and peaceful in his day, from all I hear, and he started my collection. It's a nice collection, too, blocks of four of practically every U.S. issue, first-day covers, and so on. President Roosevelt collected stamps, too, you know.

Anyway, here's what happened at Grand Central. One night last summer I worked late at the office. I was in a hurry to get uptown to my apartment so I decided to take the subway from Grand Central because it's faster than the bus.

Now, I don't know why this should have happened to me. I'm just an ordinary guy named Charley, thirty-one years old, and I was wearing a tan gabardine suit and a straw hat with a fancy band; I passed a dozen men who looked just like me. And I wasn't trying to escape from anything; I just wanted to get home to Louisa, my wife.

I turned into Grand Central from Vanderbilt Avenue, and went down the steps to the first level, where you take trains like the Twentieth Century. Then I walked down another flight to the second level, where the suburban trains leave from, ducked into an arched doorway heading for the subway—and got lost. That's easy to do. I've been in and out of Grand Central hundreds of times, but I'm always bumping into new doorways and stairs and corridors. Once I got into a tunnel about a mile long and came out in the lobby of the Roosevelt Hotel. Another time I came up in an office building on Forty-sixth Street, three blocks away.

Sometimes I think Grand Central is growing like a tree, pushing out new corridors and staircases like roots. There's probably a long tunnel that nobody knows about feeling its way under the city right now, on its way to Times Square, and maybe another to Central Park. And maybe—because for so many people through the years Grand Central *has* been an exit, a way of escape—maybe that's how the tunnel I got into . . . But I never told my psychiatrist friend about that idea.

The corridor I was in began angling left and slanting downward and I thought that was wrong, but I kept on walking. All I could hear was the empty sound of my own footsteps and I didn't pass a soul. Then I heard that sort of hollow roar ahead that means open space and people talking. The tunnel turned sharp left; I went down a short flight of stairs and came out on the third level at Grand Central Station. For just a moment I thought I was back on the second level, but I saw the room was smaller, there were fewer ticket windows and train gates, and the information booth in the center was wood and old-looking. And the man in the booth wore a green eyeshade and long black sleeve protectors. The lights were dim and sort of flickering. Then I saw why; they were open-flame gaslights.

There were brass spittoons on the floor, and across the station a glint of light caught my eye; a man was pulling a gold watch from his vest pocket. He snapped open the cover, glanced at his watch, and frowned. He wore a derby hat, a black four-buttoned suit with tiny lapels, and he had a big, black, handle-bar mustache. Then I looked around and saw that everyone in the station was dressed like eighteen-ninety-something; I never saw so many beards, sideburns and fancy mustaches in my life. A woman walked in through the train gate; she wore a dress with leg-of-mutton sleeves and skirts to the top of her high-buttoned shoes. Back of her, out on the tracks, I caught a glimpse of a locomotive, a very small Currier & Ives locomotive with a funnel-shaped stack. And then I knew.

To make sure, I walked over to a newsboy and glanced at the stack of papers at his feet. It was the *World;* and the *World* hasn't been published for years. The lead story said something about President Cleveland. I've found that front page since, in the Public Library files, and it was printed June 11, 1894.

I turned toward the ticket windows knowing that here—on the third level at Grand Central—I could buy tickets that would take Louisa and me anywhere in the United States we wanted to go. In the year 1894. And I wanted two tickets to Galesburg, Illinois.

Have you ever been there? It's a wonderful town still, with big old frame houses, huge lawns and tremendous trees whose branches meet overhead and roof the streets. And in 1894, summer evenings were twice as long, and people sat out on their lawns, the men smoking cigars and talking quietly, the women waving palm-leaf fans, with the fireflies all around, in a peaceful world. To be back there with the First World War still twenty years off, and World War II over forty years in the future ... I wanted two tickets for that.

The clerk figured the fare—he glanced at my fancy hatband, but he figured the fare—and I had enough for two coach tickets, one way. But when I counted out the money and looked up, the clerk was staring at me. He nodded at the bills. "That ain't money, mister," he said, "and if you're trying to skin me you won't get very far," and he glanced at the cash drawer beside him. Of course the money in his drawer was old-style bills, half again as big as the money we use nowadays, and different-looking. I turned away and got out fast. There's nothing nice about jail, even in 1894.

And that was that. I left the same way I came, I suppose. Next day, during lunch hour, I drew three hundred dollars out of the bank, nearly all we had, and bought old-style currency (that *really* worried my psychiatrist friend). You can buy old money at almost any coin dealer's, but you have to pay a premium. My three hundred dollars bought less than two hundred in old-style bills, but I didn't care; eggs were thirteen cents a dozen in 1894.

But I've never again found the corridor that leads to the third level at Grand Central Station, although I've tried often enough.

Louisa was pretty worried when I told her all this, and didn't want me to look for the third level any more, and after a while I stopped; I went back to my stamps. But now we're *both* looking, every week end, because now we have proof that the third level is still there. My friend Sam Weiner disappeared! Nobody knew where, but I sort of suspected because Sam's a city boy, and I used to tell him about Galesburg—I went to school there—and he always said he liked the sound of the place. And that's where he is, all right. In 1894.

Because one night, fussing with my stamp collection, I found—well, do you know what a first-day cover is? When a new stamp is issued, stamp collectors buy some and use them to mail envelopes to themselves on the very first day of sale; and the postmark proves the date. The envelope is called a first-day cover. They're never opened; you just put blank paper in the envelope.

That night, among my oldest first-day covers, I found one that shouldn't have been there. But there it was. It was there because someone had mailed it to my grandfather at his home in Galesburg; that's what the address on the envelope said. And it had been there since July 18, 1894—the postmark showed that—yet I didn't remember it at all. The stamp was a six-cent, dull brown, with a picture of President Garfield. Naturally, when the envelope came to Granddad in the mail, it went right into his collection and stayed there —till I took it out and opened it.

The paper inside wasn't blank. It read:

> *941 Willard Street*
> *Galesburg, Illinois*
> *July 18, 1894*

Charley:
I got to wishing that you were right. Then I got to believing you were right. And, Charley, it's true; I found the third level! I've been here two weeks, and right now, down the street at the Dalys', someone is playing a piano, and they're all out on the front porch singing, "Seeing Nellie home." And I'm invited over

*for lemonade. Come on back, Charley and Louisa.
Keep looking till you find the third level! It's worth
it, believe me!*

The note was signed *Sam*.

At the stamp and coin store I go to, I found out that
Sam bought eight hundred dollars' worth of old-style
currency. That ought to set him up in a nice little hay,
feed and grain business; he always said that's what he
really wished he could do, and he certainly can't go
back to his old business. Not in Galesburg, Illinois, in
1894. His old business? Why, Sam was my psychiatrist.

SUCH INTERESTING NEIGHBORS

I can't honestly say I knew from the start that there
was something queer about the Hellenbeks. I did
notice some strange things right away, and wondered
about them, but I shrugged them off. They were nice
people; I liked them; and everyone has a few odd little
tricks.

We were watching from our sun-parlor windows the
day they arrived; not snooping or prying, you understand, but naturally we were curious. Nell and I are
pretty sociable and we were hoping a couple around
our own ages would move into the new house next
door.

I was just finishing breakfast—it was a Saturday and
I wasn't working—and Nell was running the vacuum
cleaner over the sun-parlor rug. I heard the vacuum
shut off, and Nell called out, "Here they are, Al!" and
I ran in and we got our first look at the Hellenbeks.

He was helping her from a cab, and I got a good

look at him and his wife. They seemed to be just about our ages, the man maybe thirty-two or so and his wife in her middle twenties. She was rather pretty, and he had a nice, agreeable kind of face.

"Newlyweds?" Nell said, a little excited.

"Why?"

"Their clothes are all brand-new. Even the shoes. And so's the bag."

"Yeah, maybe you're right." I watched for a second or so, then said, "Foreigners, too, I think," showing Nell I was pretty observant myself.

"Why do you think so?"

"He's having trouble with the local currency." He was, too. He couldn't seem to pick out the right change, and finally he held out his hand and let the driver find the right coins.

But we were wrong on both counts. They'd been married three years, we found out later, had both been born in the States, and had lived here nearly all their lives.

Furniture deliveries began arriving next door within half an hour; everything new, all bought from local merchants. We live in San Rafael, California, in a neighborhood of small houses. Mostly young people live here, and it's a friendly, informal place. So after a while I got into an old pair of flannels and sneakers and wandered over to get acquainted and lend a hand if I could, and I cut across the two lawns. As I came up to their house, I heard them talking in the living room. "Here's a picture of Truman," he said, and I heard a newspaper rattle.

"Truman," she said, kind of thoughtfully. "Let's see now; doesn't Roosevelt come next?"

"No, Truman comes *after* Roosevelt."

"I think you're wrong, dear," she said. "It's Truman, then Roosevelt, then—"

When my feet hit their front steps, the talk stopped. At the door I knocked and glanced in; they were sitting on the living-room floor, and Ted Hellenbek was just scrambling to his feet. They'd been unpacking a carton of dishes and there was a bunch of wadded-up old newspapers lying around, and I guess they'd been looking at those. Ted came to the door. He'd changed to a T-shirt, slacks and moccasins, all brand-new.

"I'm Al Lewis from next door," I said. "Thought maybe I could give you a hand."

"Glad to know you." He pushed the door open, then stuck out his hand. "I'm Ted Hellenbek," and he grinned in a nice friendly way. His wife got up from the floor, and Ted introduced us. Her name was Ann.

Well, I worked around with them the rest of the morning, helping them unpack things, and we got the place into pretty good order. While we were working, Ted told me they'd been living in South America—he didn't say where or why—and that they'd sold everything they had down there, except the clothes they traveled in and a few personal belongings, rather than pay shipping expenses. That sounded perfectly reasonable and sensible, except that a few days later Ann told Nell their house in South America had burned down and they'd lost everything.

Maybe half an hour after I arrived, some bedding was delivered—blankets, pillows, linen, stuff like that. Ann picked up the two pillows, put cases on them, and turned toward the bedroom. Now, it was broad daylight, the bedroom door was closed, and it was made of solid wood. But Ann walked straight into that door and fell. I couldn't figure out how she came to do it; it was as though she expected the door to open by itself or something. That's what Ted said, too, going over to help her up. "Be careful, honey," he said, and laughed a little, making a joke of it. "You'll have to learn, you know, that doors won't open themselves."

Around eleven thirty or so, some books arrived, quite a slew of them, and all new. We were squatting on the floor, unpacking them, and Ted picked up a book, showed me the title, and said, "Have you read this?"

It was "The Far Reaches," by a Walter Braden. "No," I said. "I read the reviews a week or so ago, and they weren't so hot."

"I know," Ted said, and he had a funny smile on his face. "And yet it's a great book. Just think," he went on, and shook his head a little, "you can buy this now, a new copy, first edition, for three dollars. Yet in—oh, a hundred and forty years, say, a copy like this might be worth five to eight thousand dollars."

"Could be," I said, and shrugged; but what kind of a remark is that? Sure, any book you want to name might be valuable someday, but why *that* book? And why a hundred and forty years? And why five to eight thousand dollars, particularly? Well, that's the kind of thing I mean about the Hellenbeks. It wasn't that anything big or dramatic or really out of the way happened that first day. It was just that every once in a while one or the other would do or say something that wasn't quite right.

Most of the time, though, things were perfectly ordinary and normal. We talked and laughed and kidded around a lot, and I knew I was going to like the Hellenbeks and that Nelly would, too.

In the afternoon we got pretty hot and thirsty, so I went home and brought back some beer. This time Nelly came with me, met the new people, and invited them over for supper. Nelly complimented Ann on the nice things she had, and Ann thanked her and apologized, the way a woman will, because things were kind of dusty. Then she went out to the kitchen, came back with a dustcloth, and started dusting around. It was a white cloth with a small green pattern, and it got pretty dirty, and when she wiped off the window sills it was really streaked.

Then Ann leaned out the front window, shook the cloth once, and—it was clean again. I mean *completely* clean; the dirt, every trace of it, shook right out. She did that several times, dusting around the room and then shaking the cloth out, and it shook out white every time.

Well, Nelly sat there with her mouth hanging open, and finally she said, "Where in the world did you get that dustcloth?"

Ann glanced down at the cloth in her hand, then looked up at Nelly again and said, "Why, it's just an old rag, from one of Ted's old suits." Then suddenly she blushed.

I'd have blushed, too; did you ever see a man's suit, white with a little green pattern?

Nell said, "Well, I never saw a dustcloth before that would shake out perfectly clean. Mine certainly don't."

Ann turned even redder, looking absolutely confused, and—I'd say *scared*. She mumbled something about cloth in South América, glanced at Ted, and then put the back of her wrist up against her forehead, and for an instant I'd have sworn she was going to cry.

But Ted got up fast, put his arm around Ann's waist and turned her a little so her back was toward us, and said something about how she'd been working too hard and was tired. His eyes, though, as he stood looking at us over Ann's shoulder, were hard and defiant. For a moment you almost got the feeling that it was the two of them against the world, that Ted was protecting Ann against us.

Then Nelly ran a hand admiringly over the top of the end table beside her and said how much she liked it, and Ann turned and smiled and thanked her. Nelly got up and led Ann off to the bedroom, telling her not to try to do too much all in one day, and when they came out a little later everything was all right.

We got to know the Hellenbeks pretty well. They were casual, easygoing, and always good company. In no time Nelly and Ann were doing their marketing together, dropping in on each other during the day, and trading recipes.

At night, out watering our lawns or cutting the grass or something, Ted and I would usually bat the breeze about one thing or another till it got dark. We talked politics, high prices, gardening, stuff like that. He knew plenty about politics and world events, and it was surprising the way his predictions would turn out. At first I offered to bet with him about a few things we disagreed about, but he never would and I'm glad he didn't; he was seldom wrong when it came to guessing what was going to happen.

Well, that's the way things were. We'd drop in on each other, take Sunday drives together and go on picnics, play a little bridge at night and on week ends.

Odd little things would still happen occasionally, but less and less often as time went by—and none of them were ever repeated. When Ted bought something now, he never had trouble finding the right change, and he didn't discover any more rare old new books, and Ann stopped walking into doors.

They were always interesting neighbors, though. For one thing, Ted was an inventor. I don't know why that should have surprised me, but it did. There are such things as inventors; they have to live somewhere, and there's no good reason why one shouldn't move in next door to us. But Ted didn't *seem* like an in-

ventor; why, the first time he cut their grass, I had to
show him how to adjust the set screw that keeps the
blades in alignment.

But just the same he was an inventor and a good
one. One evening I was picking tomatoes in the little
garden we have, and Ted wandered over, tossing
something into the air and catching it again. I thought
it was a paper clip at first. Ted stood watching me for a
minute or so, and then he squatted down beside me
and held out this thing in his hand and said, "Ever
see anything like this before?"

I took it and looked at it; it was a piece of thin wire
bent at each end to form two egg-shaped loops. Then
the wire had been bent again at the middle so that the
two loops slid together. I can't explain it very well,
but I could make you one easy in half a minute. "What
is it?" I said, and handed it back to him.

"A little invention—the Saf-T-Clip," he said. "You
use it wherever you'd ordinarily use a safety pin.
Here." He unbuttoned one of my shirt buttons and
slid the thing onto the two layers of cloth.

Well, do you know that I couldn't unfasten my shirt
where that little thing gripped it? Even when I took
hold of both sides of my shirt and pulled, that little
piece of twisted wire just dug in and held. Yet when
Ted showed me how to undo it—you just pressed the
wire at a certain place—it slid right off. It was just
the kind of simple thing you wonder, "Now, why didn't
somebody ever think of that before?"

I told Ted I thought it was a hell of a good idea.
"How'd you happen to think of it?" I asked.

He smiled. "Oh, it was surprisingly easy. That's
how I'm planning to make a living, Al—inventing little
things. First thing I did, the day we arrived in San
Rafael, was get a patent application sent off on this
thing. Then I mailed a sample to a wire company." He

grinned happily and said, "I got a reply today; they'll buy it outright for fifteen hundred dollars."

"You going to take it?"

"Sure. I don't think it's the best offer in the world and I might do better if I shopped around. But I've been a little worried, frankly, about how we were going to pay for the furniture and stuff we bought, and the house rent." He shrugged. "So I'm glad to get this money. We'll be okay, now, till I finish the next project."

"What's the next one?" I said. "If you can tell me, that is." I set the tomatoes down and sat down on the grass.

"Sure, I can tell you," he said. "Picture a flashlight with a little dial set in just above the button. There's a lens, but it curves inward, and it's painted black except for a tiny round hole in the center. Press the button and a little beam of light—a special *kind* of light—no thicker than a pencil lead, shoots out. The beam doesn't spread, either; it stays the same thickness. You get the idea?"

"Yeah. What's it for?"

"For measuring distances. Turn it on, aim the little dot of light so it hits the end of any distance you want to measure. Then look at the dial, and you can read off the distance from the dot of light to the edge of the lens in feet and fractions of an inch, down to sixteenths." He smiled. "Sound good?"

"Hell, yes," I said. "But how will it work?"

"On flashlight batteries," Ted said, and stood up, as if that were an answer.

Well, I took the hint and didn't ask any more questions, but if he can make a thing like that—a guy who had to have help adjusting his lawn mower—then I'll eat it when he's finished. And yet, darned if I don't think, sometimes, that he might do it at that.

Oh, Hellenbek's an interesting guy, all right. Told me once that in fifty years they'd be growing full-grown trees from seeds in ten days' time. Indoors, too, and with absolutely straight grain and no knots; regular wood factories. I asked him what made him think so and he shrugged and said it was just an idea he had. But you see what I mean; the Hellenbeks were interesting neighbors.

I guess the most interesting time we ever spent with them, though, was one evening on our front porch. Supper was over, and I was reading a magazine that had come in the mail that morning. Nell was on the porch swing, knitting. The magazine I was reading was all science fiction—trips to Mars in space ships, gun fights with atomic pistols, and so on. I get a kick out of that kind of stuff, though Nell thinks it's silly.

Pretty soon the Hellenbeks wandered over. Ann sat down with Nelly, and Ted leaned on the porch rail, facing my chair. "What're you reading?" he said, nodding at the magazine in my lap.

I handed it to him, a little embarrassed. The cover illustration showed a man from Jupiter with eyes on the ends of long tentacles. "Don't know if you ever read this kind of stuff or not," I said.

Ann said to Nell, "I tried that biscuit mix. It's wonderful."

"Oh, did you like it?" Nell was pleased, and they started talking food and cooking.

Ted began leafing through my magazine, and I lighted a cigarette and just sat there looking out at the street, feeling lazy and comfortable. It was a nice night, and still pretty light out. Ted got very quiet, slowly turning the pages, studying the illustrations, reading a paragraph or so here and there, and once he said, "Well, I'll be damned," sort of half under his breath.

He must have looked through that magazine for ten

minutes or more, and I could tell he was fascinated. Finally he looked up, handed the magazine back, and said, kind of surprised, "That's very interesting, really very interesting."

"Yeah, some of the science-fiction stuff is pretty good," I said. "There was a magazine story not long ago, by Ray Bradbury. About a man of the future who escapes back to our times. But then the secret police of the future come for him and take him back."

"Really?" Ted said. "I missed that."

"It might be around the house. If I find it, I'll give it to you."

"I'd like to see it," he said. I had the impression that that sort of thing was brand-new to Ted, but I was wrong because then he said, "Now that I know you're interested—" For just a moment he hesitated; then he went on, "Well, the fact is I wrote a science-fiction story myself once."

Ann glanced up quickly, the way a woman does when her husband gets off on the wrong subject. Then she turned back to Nell, smiling and nodding, but I could tell she was listening to Ted. "Yeah?" I said.

"Yeah. I worked out this story on the world of the future that you—"

"Ted!" said Ann.

But he just grinned at her and went on talking to me. "Ann's always afraid I'll bore people with some of my ideas."

"Well, this one's *silly,*" Ann said.

"Of course it is," Nell said, soothing her down. "I can't understand why Al reads that sort of thing."

"Well, you gals just go on with your talk, then," Ted said. "You don't have to listen. Honey," he said to Ann, "this is different; this is all right."

"Sure," I said, "it's harmless. At least we're not out drinking or hanging around the pool hall."

"Well . . ." He shifted his position and was smiling, very eager, almost excited. I could tell this was something he was itching to talk about. "A friend of mine and I used to bat the breeze around about this kind of stuff, and we worked out a story. Matter of fact, we did more than that. He was an amateur printer; had his own printing press in the basement. Did beautiful work. So one time, just for a gag, we printed up an article, a magazine, the way it might look and read sometime in the future. I've still got a copy or two around somewhere. Like to see it?"

"Ted," Ann said pleadingly.

"It's all *right,* honey," he said.

Well, of course I said sure, I'd like to see his article, and Ted went on over to their house and in a minute or so he came back with a long narrow strip of paper and handed it to me.

It didn't feel like paper when I took it; it was almost like fine linen to the touch, and it didn't rattle or crackle, but it was stiff like paper. At the top of the page, there was a title, printed in red—long thin letters, but very easy to read. It said: Time on Our Hands? Underneath was a caption: *Should TT be outlawed? A grave new question facing a world already stunned with fear of oxygen-reversion, population-deterrent and "crazy-molecule" weapons.*

Ted said, "The funny shape of the page is because that's how it comes out of the teleprint receivers in subscribers' homes."

Both the girls looked at him contemptuously, and went on with their conversation.

"Pretty elaborate gag," I said.

"I know," he said, and laughed. "We spent a lot of time fooling around with that thing."

I turned back to the article, and a picture in the middle of the page caught my eye. It was a man's face, smiling, and it seemed to stick right out of the page. It was taken full face, yet you could see the nose jutting out at you, and the ears and sides of the head seemed farther back in the page. It was beautifully printed and in marvelous color. You could see fine lines around the eyes, the film of moisture on the eyeballs, and every separate strand of hair. I raised the picture closer to my eyes and it went flat, two-dimensional, and I could see it was printed, all right. But when I lowered it to reading distance again, the photograph popped out in three dimensions once more, a perfect miniature human face.

The caption said: *Ralph Kent, thirty-two-year-old quantum physicist and world's first Time-Traveler. His initial words upon his reappearance in the laboratory after testing TT are now world-famous. "Nobody in sixteenth-century England," he announced, "seems to understand English."*

"Your friend does some pretty fine printing," I said to Ted.

"The photograph?" he said. "Oh, you can get results like that if you're willing to take the time. Go ahead; read the article."

I lighted another cigarette and started to read. The article said:

The first practical Time-machine reached blueprint stage in the Schenectady laboratories of the DeFarday Electric Company in November of last year, a closely guarded secret among seven top officials of the company. It is said to have been based on an extension of the basic theories of Albert Einstein, famous theoretical physicist of the last century.

A handmade pilot model of DE's astounding invention was completed on May 18th of this year at a cost, excluding four years' preliminary research expense, of approximately $190,000. But even before it was com-

pleted and successfully tested, it was out of date. A young Australian physicist, Finis Bride, of the University of Melbourne, had published accounts of experiments in which he had successfully substituted a cheaply maintained electric flow-field for the conventional and expensive platinum-alloy heretofore used in gravity-repulsion. The way was cleared, as DE officials were quick to realize, for inexpensive mass production of Time-machines.

It was vitally important, DE's board decided, to try to keep the young Australian's invention a secret from competitors. But almost inevitably, while DE was in the process of tooling up, the secret leaked, and soon Asco, BCA and Eastern Electric were in the race to hit the market first. Almost as quickly, British, French, Russian, Italian, and, soon after, televip manufacturers throughout the entire world were in the scramble. By June of this year TT sets were selling at the rate . . .

Ted's article went on like that. It was really cleverly done. There were times when you'd almost think you were reading the real McCoy. It told how Time-Travel sets hit the market with a big advertising splash early in the summer. The first day they went on sale the public was apathetic and skeptical. But the following day the press and the televip networks (whatever they were supposed to be) were filled with interviews with people who'd tried Time-Travel, and they were all absolutely bug-eyed with astonishment because the damned machine actually worked.

You put a little gadget in your pocket called a "tampered relay." Then you turned on your set, adjusted the dials, stepped into a little beam of invisible light, and you'd appear instantly at just about any time and place you'd set the dials for. You left the set on, or adjusted it to turn on automatically after a certain length of time, and as long as you still had your "tampered relay" all you had to do was stand in the same spot you'd first appeared in and you'd be right back home again standing in the beam of invisible light. Well, the public went nuts for it, and at the time the article was supposedly written, production was going full blast, twenty-four hours a day, and practically every last family in the country was scraping up at least the hundred and fifty dollars which the cheapest model cost.

It was really an imaginative job. One of the neatest touches about it was the note of worry that ran all through the article. It was as though there were some awful problem connected with this rage for Time-Travel that the author didn't quite want to put into words. He kept hinting about it, wondering if new legislation weren't needed, and so on, but I couldn't quite figure out what he was supposed to be bothered about. Time-Travel sounded like a lot of fun to me.

"That's a wonderful job," I told Ted when I finished. "But what's the point? All that trouble—for what?"

Ted shrugged. "I don't know," he said. "No point, I guess. Did you like it?"

"I sure did."

"You can have that copy if you want. I've got another."

"Thanks," I said, and laid it in my lap. "But what did you plan to have happen next?"

"Oh," he said, "you don't want to hear any more." He seemed a little embarrassed, as though he wished he hadn't started this, and he glanced over at his wife, but she wouldn't look at him. "Matter of fact," he went on, "the story sort of peters out. I'm really not very good at that kind of thing."

"Yes," said Ann, "that's enough."

"Come on," I said to Ted. "Give."

Ted looked at me for a moment, very serious, then he shook his head again. "No," he said, "it's too hard to explain. You'd have to know a good deal about a world of the future, a world in which people are sick with the fear of self-destruction. Unimaginable weapons that could literally tear the entire solar system to pieces. Everyone living in absolute dread of the future."

"What's so hard to imagine about that?"

"Oh, hell"—he laughed. "These are peaceful times."

"They are?"

"Sure. No weapon worth mentioning except the atom and hydrogen bombs, and those in their earliest, uncomplex stages."

I laughed kind of sourly.

"All in all," he said, "these are pretty nice times to be alive in."

"Well, I'm glad you're so sure," I said.

"I am," Ted answered, and he smiled. Then he stopped smiling. "But it'll be different in another century or so, believe me. At least," he added, "that's how this friend and I figured it out in our story." He shook his head a little and went on, sort of talking to himself.

"Life will barely be worth living. Everyone working twelve, fourteen hours a day, with the major part of a man's income going for taxes, and the rest going for consumers' goods priced sky-high because of war production. Artificial scarcities, restrictions of all kinds. And hanging over everything, killing what little joy in life is left, is the virtual certainty of death and destruction. Everyone working and sacrificing for his own destruction." Ted looked up at me. "A lousy world, the world of the future, and not the way human beings were meant to live."

"Go ahead," I said, "you're doing fine."

He grinned, looked at me for a moment, then

shrugged. "Okay," he said, and settled back on the porch rail. "Time-Travel hits the world the way television has hit the country today, only it happens a hundred times faster, because it's just about the only way to have any real fun. But it's a wonderful way, all right. Within less than a week after the first sets reach the market, people everywhere are going swimming after work on an untouched beach in California, say in the year 1000. Or fishing or picnicking in the Maine woods before even the Norsemen had arrived. Or standing on a hill overlooking a battlefield, watching the Crusaders have it out with the infidels."

Ted smiled. "But sometimes it's not too safe. In Newton, Kansas, a man arrives home in his living room, bleeding to death from arrow wounds. In Tallahassee a whole family disappears, their TT set turned on and humming, and they are never heard from again, and the same thing happens here and there all over the country and the world. In Chicago a man returns from a day in seventh-century France and dies in two days of the plague; everyone is worried stiff, but the disease doesn't spread. In Mill Valley, California, a man reappears in his home, his face gashed, his hand mangled, his clothes torn to shreds, and he commits suicide the following day. His wife has been stoned to death as a witch because they were fools enough to appear in a crowded eleventh-century Danish public square in modern dress, talking twenty-first-century English."

Ted grinned and winked at his wife; he was enjoying himself. I was fascinated and I think Nell was, too, whether she'd admit it or not. "But then," he went on, "warnings are soon published and televipped by all the TT manufacturers and by the government, too, and people quickly learn caution. Brief courses of instruction are published on how to conduct oneself in various times, how to simulate the dress and customs of earlier periods, what dangerous times and places to avoid, and TT really comes into its own. There are still risks, still accidents and tragedies, of course.

"Inevitably some people talk too much—the temptation is terribly strong—and they land in insane asylums or jails. Others can't stay away from the danger times and are lynched by superstitious mobs. A good many people die of the common cold, which science had eradicated and to which the human race had lost its old resistance. But there's risk in anything, and the important thing is that once again it's possible to take a *vacation*. To really get away from it all for a week, a day, or even an hour before dinner. To go back to simpler, more peaceful times when life is worth living again. And nearly every last soul in the world soon finds a way somehow to own a TT set or get access to one."

Ted looked at me, then at Nell. "Naturally, then, the inevitable happened; the only possible ending to my story. Maybe you've figured out what had to happen?"

I shook my head, and Ted looked at Nell to see if she knew; then he said, "It's easy. People simply stopped coming back. All over the world, within less than a month after TT is introduced, the same almost simultaneous thought seems to strike everyone: Why return? By this time everyone has discovered a favorite time and place in the history and geography of the world. And everybody is enthusiastic for his own particular discovery; some one century or decade, some country, city, town, island, woods or seashore, some one spot on the world's surface at a certain time that best suits his temperament. And so the same inspiration hits nearly everyone: Why not *stay* there? Why come back? To what?"

Ted slapped at a stray mosquito and said, "Within forty days' time the population of the entire world is down to less than seven million people, and nearly all of them are getting ready to leave. Suddenly the world is left to the tiny fraction of one per cent of human beings who want wars and who cause them. But the people who fight them walk out. Before the governments of the world realize what's happening—before there's time to do anything about it—the world's population is nearly gone.

"The last emergency Cabinet meeting of the U.S. government breaks up when the assembled members discover that all but one of them are themselves planning to leave for other times. In six more days the twenty-first century is deserted like a sinking ship, its population scattered thinly back through the preceding twenty-five hundred years. And of the very few who are finally left—the tiny minority who preferred the present —most are soon forced, out of sheer loneliness and the breakdown of a world, to join friends and families in earlier times."

Ted looked at us for a moment, then said, "And that, my friends, is how the world ends. On the edge of a precipice, with one foot over the edge, it stops, turns and goes back, leaving an empty earth of birds and insects, wind, rain and rusting weapons."

For maybe half a minute Ted sat staring at nothing, and no one said anything; a cricket began to chirp feebly off in the grass somewhere. Then Ted smiled. "Well," he said, "how do you like it, Al? Good story?"

"Yeah," I said slowly, still thinking about it. "Yeah," I said, "I like it fine. Why don't you write it; maybe get it published somewhere?"

"Well, I thought about that, as a matter of fact, but on the whole I prefer inventing. It's easier."

"Well, it's a good story," I said, "though there are some flaws in it of course."

"I'm sure of it," Ted said, "but what are they?"

"Well, for one thing, wouldn't people in those earlier times notice the sudden increase in population?"

"I don't think so. Spread the world's population through the thousands of preceding years, and at any one time or place it wouldn't be more than a drop in the bucket."

"Okay," I said, "but speaking of inventions, wouldn't everyone traveling back to simpler times start introducing twenty-first century inventions?"

"Not to amount to anything. You mean like space ships in seventeen seventy-six?"

"Something like that."

Ted shook his head. "It couldn't happen. Suppose *you* went back a hundred years; could you make a television set?"

"No."

"Or even a radio?"

"I might. A simple one, anyway. Maybe a crystal set."

"All right," Ted said, "suppose you did. I doubt if you could find all the materials—copper wire, for example—but suppose you managed; what would you listen to? You'd tell people it was a radio and what it was for, and they'd lock you up. You see? And what do most people know anyway about the marvelous things they use every day? Practically nothing. And even the few who do know could never find what they'd need to duplicate them, except in the actual time they belong in. The best you could do would be to introduce one or two of the very simplest things people used in your time, like a modern safety pin in Elizabethan England, if you could find the steel. And a few things like that wouldn't upset the history of the world.

"No, Al, you'd just have to take your place as best you could in the world as you found it, no matter what you knew about the future."

Well, I let it go at that. I didn't mean to get started knocking holes in Ted's story, and I went into the house and broke out beer for all hands. I liked Ted's story, though, and so did Nell, and we both said so, and after a while even Ann broke down and said she liked it, too. Then the conversation got off onto other things.

But there you are. It's like I said the Hellenbeks were strange in some ways, but very interesting neighbors, and I was sorry to see them move away. They moved not too long afterward. They liked California fine, they said, and liked the people they'd met. But they were lonesome for old friends, people they'd grown up with, and that's understandable, of course.

So they moved to Orange, New Jersey. Some old friends were arriving there soon, they said, and the Hellenbeks were anxious to be with them. They expected them, Ted told me, sometime in the spring of 1958, and they wanted to be on hand to meet them.

There's a new couple next door now—perfectly nice people who play a good game of bridge, and we like them okay. But I don't know; after the Hellenbeks, they seem kind of dull.

I'M SCARED

I'm very badly scared, not so much for myself—I'm a gray-haired man of sixty-six, after all—but for you and everyone else who has not yet lived out his life. For I believe that certain dangerous things have recently begun to happen in the world. They are noticed here and there, idly discussed, then dismissed and forgotten.

Yet I am convinced that unless these occurrences are recognized for what they are, the world will be plunged into a nightmare. Judge for yourself.

One evening last winter I came home from a chess club to which I belong. I'm a widower; I live alone in a small but comfortable three-room apartment overlooking lower Fifth Avenue. It was still fairly early, and I switched on a lamp beside my leather easy chair, picked up a murder mystery I'd been reading, and turned on the radio; I did not, I'm sorry to say, notice which station it was tuned to.

The tubes warmed, and the music of an accordion—faint at first, then louder—came from the loud-speaker. Since it was good music for reading, I adjusted the volume control and began to read.

Now, I want to be absolutely factual and accurate about this, and I do not claim that I paid close attention to the radio. But I do know that presently the music stopped, and an audience applauded. Then a man's voice, chuckling and pleased with the applause, said, "All right, all right," but the applause continued for several more seconds. During that time the voice once more chuckled appreciatively, then firmly repeated, "All right," and the applause died down. "That was Alec Somebody-or-other," the radio voice said, and I went back to my book.

But I soon became aware of this middle-aged voice again; perhaps a change of tone as he turned to a new subject caught my attention. "And now, Miss Ruth Greeley," he was saying, "of Trenton, New Jersey. Miss Greeley is a pianist; that right?" A girl's voice, timid and barely audible, said, "That's right, Major Bowes." The man's voice—and now I recognized his familiar singsong delivery—said, "And what are you going to play?" The girl replied, "La Paloma." The man repeated it after her, as an announcement: "La Paloma."

There was a pause, then an introductory chord sounded from a piano, and I resumed my reading.

As the girl played, I was half aware that her style was mechanical, her rhythm defective; perhaps she was nervous. Then my attention was fully aroused once more by a gong which sounded suddenly. For a few notes more the girl continued to play falteringly, not sure what to do. The gong sounded jarringly again, the playing abruptly stopped, and there was a restless murmur from the audience. "All right, all right," said the now familiar voice, and I realized I'd been expecting this, knowing it would say just that. The audience quieted, and the voice began, "Now—"

The radio went dead. For the smallest fraction of a second no sound issued from it but its own mechanical hum. Then a completely different program came from the loud-speaker; the recorded voice of Andy Williams singing, "You Butterfly," a favorite of mine. So I returned once more to my reading, wondering vaguely what had happened to the other program, but not actually thinking about it until I finished my book and began to get ready for bed.

Then, undressing in my bedroom, I remembered that Major Bowes was dead. Years had passed, a decade, since that dry chuckle and familiar, "All right, all right," had been heard in the nation's living rooms.

Well, what does one do when the apparently impossible occurs? It simply made a good story to tell friends, and more than once I was asked if I'd recently heard Moran and Mack, a pair of radio comedians popular some thirty years ago, or Floyd Gibbons, an old-time news broadcaster. And there were other joking references to my crystal radio set.

But one man—this was at a lodge meeting the following Thursday—listened to my story with utter seriousness, and when I had finished he told me a queer little story of his own. He is a thoughtful, intelligent man, and as I listened I was not frightened, but puzzled at what seemed to be a connecting link, a common denominator, between this story and the odd behavior of my radio. The following day, since I am retired and have plenty of time, I took the trouble of making a two-hour train trip to Connecticut in order to verify the story at first hand. I took detailed notes, and the story appears in my files now as follows:

Case 2. Louis Trachnor, coal and wood dealer, R.F.D. 1, Danbury, Connecticut, aged fifty-four.

On July 20, 1956, Mr. Trachnor told me, he walked out on the front porch of his house about six o'clock in the morning. Running from the eaves of his house to the floor of the porch was a streak of gray paint, still damp. "It was about the width of an eight-inch brush," Mr. Trachnor told me, "and it looked like hell, because the house was white. I figured some kids did it in the night for a joke, but if they did, they had to get a ladder up to the eaves and you wouldn't figure they'd go to that much trouble. It wasn't smeared, either; it was a careful job, a nice even stripe straight down the front of the house."

Mr. Trachnor got a ladder and cleaned off the gray paint with turpentine.

In October of that same year, Mr. Trachnor painted his house. "The white hadn't held up so good, so I painted it gray. I got to the front last and finished about five one Saturday afternoon. Next morning when I came out, I saw a streak of white right down the front of the house. I figured it was the damned kids again, because it was the same place as before. But when I looked close, I saw it wasn't new paint; it was the old white I'd painted over. Somebody had done a nice careful job of cleaning off the new paint in a long stripe about eight inches wide right down from the eaves! Now, who the hell would go to that trouble? I just can't figure it out."

Do you see the link between this story and mine? Suppose for a moment that something had happened, on each occasion, to disturb briefly the orderly progress of time. That seemed to have happened in my case; for a matter of some seconds I apparently heard a radio broadcast that had been made years before. Suppose, then, that no one had touched Mr. Trachnor's house but himself; that he had painted his house in October, and that through some fantastic mix-up in time, a portion of that paint appeared on his house the previous summer. Since he had cleaned the paint off at that time, a broad stripe of new gray paint was missing *after* he painted his house in the fall.

I would be lying, however, if I said I really believed this. It was merely an intriguing speculation, and I told both these little stories to friends, simply as curious anecdotes. I am a sociable person, see a good many people, and occasionally I heard other odd stories in response to mine.

Someone would nod and say, "Reminds me of something I heard recently . . ." and I would have one more to add to my collection. A man on Long Island received a telephone call from his sister in New York on Friday evening. She insists that she did not make this call until the following Monday, three days later. At the Forty-fifth Street branch of the Chase National Bank, I was shown a check deposited the day before it was written. A letter was delivered on East Sixty-eighth Street in New York City, just seventeen minutes after it was dropped into a mailbox on the main street of Green River, Wyoming.

And so on, and so on; my stories were now in demand at parties, and I told myself that collecting and

verifying them was a hobby. But the day I heard Julia
Eisenberg's story, I knew it was no longer that.

*Case 17. Julia Eisenberg, office worker, New York
City, aged thirty-one.*

Miss Eisenberg lives in a small walk-up apartment in
Greenwich Village. I talked to her there after a chess-
club friend who lives in her neighborhood had repeated to me a somewhat garbled version of her story,
which was told to him by the doorman of the building
he lives in.

In October, 1954, about eleven at night, Miss Eisenberg left her apartment to walk to the drugstore for
toothpaste. On her way back, not far from her apartment, a large black and white dog ran up to her and
put his front paws on her chest.

"I made the mistake of petting him," Miss Eisenberg told me, "and from then on he simply wouldn't
leave. When I went into the lobby of my building, I
actually had to push him away to get the door closed.
I felt sorry for him, poor hound, and a little guilty,
because he was still sitting at the door an hour later
when I looked out my front window."

This dog remained in the neighborhood for three
days, discovering and greeting Miss Eisenberg with
wild affection each time she appeared on the street.
"When I'd get on the bus in the morning to go to
work, he'd sit on the curb looking after me in the
most mournful way, poor thing. I wanted to take him
in, and I wish with all my heart that I had, but I knew
he'd never go home then, and I was afraid whoever
owned him would be sorry to lose him. No one in the
neighborhood knew who he belonged to, and finally
he disappeared."

Two years later a friend gave Miss Eisenberg a three-
week-old puppy. "My apartment is really too small for
a dog, but he was such a darling I couldn't resist. Well,

he grew up into a big dog who ate more than I did."

Since the neighborhood was quiet, and the dog well behaved, Miss Eisenberg usually unleashed him when she walked him at night, for he never strayed far. "One night—I'd last seen him sniffing around in the dark a few doors down—I called to him and he didn't come back. And he never did; I never saw him again.

"Now, our street is a solid wall of brownstone buildings on both sides, with locked doors and no areaways. He *couldn't* have disappeared like that, he just *couldn't*. But he did."

Miss Eisenberg hunted for her dog for many days afterward, inquired of neighbors, put ads in the papers, but she never found him. "Then one night I was getting ready for bed; I happened to glance out the front window down at the street, and suddenly I remembered something I'd forgotten all about. I remembered the dog I'd chased away over two years before." Miss Eisenberg looked at me for a moment, then she said flatly, "It was the same dog. If you own a dog you *know* him, you can't be mistaken, and I tell you it was the same dog. Whether it makes sense or not, my dog was lost—I chased him away—two years before he was born.".

She began to cry silently, the tears running down her face. "Maybe you think I'm crazy, or a little lonely and overly sentimental about a dog. But you're wrong." She brushed at her tears with a handkerchief. "I'm a well-balanced person, as much as anyone is these days, at least, and I tell you I *know* what happened."

It was in that moment, sitting in Miss Eisenberg's neat, shabby living room, that I realized fully that the consequences of these odd little incidents could be something more than merely intriguing; that they might, quite possibly, be tragic. It was in that moment that I began to be afraid.

I have spent the last eleven months discovering and tracking down these strange occurrences, and I am astonished and frightened at how many there are. I am astonished and frightened at how much more frequently they are happening now, and—I hardly know how to express this—at their increasing *power* to tear human lives tragically apart. This is an example, selected almost at random, of the increasing strength of—whatever it is that is happening in the world.

Case 34. Paul V. Kerch, accountant, the Bronx, aged thirty-one.

On a bright, clear, Sunday afternoon, I met an unsmiling family of three at their Bronx apartment: Mr. Kerch, a chunky, darkly good-looking young man; his wife, a pleasant-faced dark-haired woman in her late twenties, whose attractiveness was marred by circles under her eyes; and their son, a nice-looking boy of six or seven. After introductions, the boy was sent to his room at the back of the house to play.

"All right," Mr. Kerch said wearily then, and walked toward a bookcase, "let's get at it. You said on the phone that you know the story in general." It was half a question, half a statement.

"Yes," I said.

He took a book from the top shelf and removed some photographs from it. "There are the pictures." He sat down on the davenport beside me, with the photographs in his hand. "I own a pretty good camera, I'm a fair amateur photographer, and I have a darkroom setup in the kitchen; do my own developing. Two weeks ago, we went down to Central Park." His voice was a tired monotone as though this were a story he'd repeated many times, aloud and in his own mind. "It was nice, like today, and the kid's grandmothers have been pestering us for pictures, so I took a whole roll of films, pictures of all of us. My camera can be set up and focused and it will snap the picture automatically a few seconds later, giving me time to get around in front of it and get in the picture myself."

There was a tired, hopeless look in his eyes as he handed me all but one of the photographs. "These are the first ones I took," he said. The photographs were all fairly large, perhaps 5 × 7", and I examined them closely.

They were ordinary enough, very sharp and detailed, and each showed the family of three in various smiling poses. Mr. Kerch wore a light business suit, his wife had on a dark dress and a cloth coat, and the boy wore a dark suit with knee-length pants. In the background stood a tree with bare branches. I glanced up at Mr. Kerch, signifying that I had finished my study of the photographs.

"The last picture," he said, holding it in his hand ready to give to me, "I took exactly like the others. We agreed on the pose, I set the camera, walked around in front, and joined my family. Monday night I developed the whole roll. This is what came out on the last negative." He handed me the photograph.

For an instant it seemed to me like merely one more photograph in the group; then I saw the difference. Mr. Kerch looked much the same, bare-headed and grinning broadly, but he wore an entirely different suit. The boy, standing beside him, wore long pants, was a good three inches taller, obviously older, but equally obviously the same boy. The woman was an entirely different person. Dressed smartly, her light hair catching the sun, she was very pretty and attractive, and she was smiling into the camera, holding Mr. Kerch's hand. I looked up at him. "Who is this?"

Wearily, Mr. Kerch shook his head. "I don't know," he said sullenly, then suddenly exploded: "I don't *know!* I've never seen her in my life!" He turned to look at his wife, but she would not return his glance, and he turned back to me, shrugging. "Well, there you have it," he said. "The whole story." And he stood up, thrusting both hands into his trouser pockets, and began to pace about the room, glancing often at his wife, talking to *her* actually, though he addressed his words to me. "So who is she? How could the camera have snapped that picture? I've never seen that woman in my life!"

I glanced at the photograph again, then bent closer. "The trees here are in full bloom," I said. Behind the solemn-faced boy, the grinning man and smiling woman, the trees of Central Park were in full summer leaf.

Mr. Kerch nodded. "I know," he said bitterly. "And you know what *she* says?" he burst out, glaring at his wife. "She says that *is* my wife in the photograph, my *new* wife a couple of years from now! God!" He slapped both hands down on his head. "The ideas a woman can get!"

"What do you mean?" I glanced at Mrs. Kerch, but she ignored me, remaining silent, her lips tight.

Kerch shrugged hopelessly. "She says that photograph shows how things will be a couple of years from now. She'll be dead or"—he hesitated, then said the word bitterly—"divorced, and I'll have our son and be married to the woman in the picture."

We both looked at Mrs. Kerch, waiting until she was obliged to speak.

"Well, if it isn't so," she said, shrugging a shoulder, "then tell me what that picture does mean."

Neither of us could answer that, and a few minutes later I left. There was nothing much I could say to the Kerches; certainly I couldn't mention my conviction that, whatever the explanation of the last photograph, their married life was over. . . .

Case 72. Lieutenant Alfred Eichler, New York Police Department, aged thirty-three.

In the late evening of January 9, 1956, two policemen found a revolver lying just off a gravel path near an East Side entrance to Central Park. The gun was examined for fingerprints at the police laboratory and several were found. One bullet had been fired from the revolver and the police fired another which was studied and classified by a ballistics expert. The fingerprints were checked and found in police files; they were those of a minor hoodlum with a record of assault.

A routine order to pick him up was sent out. A detective called at the rooming house where he was known to live, but he was out, and since no unsolved shootings had occurred recently, no intensive search for him was made that night.

The following evening a man was shot and killed in Central Park with the same gun. This was proved ballistically past all question of error. It was soon learned that the murdered man had been quarreling with a friend in a nearby tavern. The two men, both drunk, had left the tavern together. And the second man was the hoodlum whose gun had been found the previous night, and which was still locked in a police safe. As Lieutenant Eichler said to me, "It's impossible that the dead man was killed with that same gun, but he was. Don't ask me how, though, and if anybody thinks we'd go into court with a case like that, they're crazy."

Case 111. Captain Hubert V. Rihm, New York Police Department, retired, aged sixty-six.

I met Captain Rihm by appointment one morning in Stuyvesant Park, a patch of greenery, wood benches and asphalt surrounded by the city, on lower Second Avenue. "You want to hear about the Fentz case, do you?" he said, after we had introduced ourselves and found an empty bench. "All right, I'll tell you. I don't like to talk about it—it bothers me—but I'd like to see what you think." He was a big, rather heavy man, with a red, tough face, and he wore an old police jacket and uniform cap with the insigne removed.

"I was up at City Mortuary," he began, as I took out my notebook and pencil, "at Bellevue, about twelve one night, drinking coffee with one of the interns. This was in June, 1955, just before I retired, and I was in Missing Persons. They brought this guy in and he was a funny-looking character. Had a beard. A young guy, maybe thirty, but he wore regular muttonchop whiskers, and his clothes were funny-looking. Now, I was thirty years on the force and I've seen a lot of queer guys killed on the streets. We found an Arab once, in full regalia, and it took us a week to find out who he was. So it wasn't just the way the guy looked that bothered me; it was the stuff we found in his pockets."

Captain Rihm turned on the bench to see if he'd caught my interest, then continued. "There was about a dollar in change in the dead guy's pocket, and one of the boys picked up a nickel and showed it to me. Now, you've seen plenty of nickels, the new ones with Jefferson's picture, the buffalo nickels they made before that, and once in a while you still see even the old Liberty-head nickels; they quit making them before the First World War. But this one was even older than that. It had a shield on the front, a U.S. shield, and a big five on the back; I used to see that kind when I was a boy. And the funny thing was, that old nickel looked new; what coin dealers call 'mint condition,' like it was made the day before yesterday. The date on that nickel was 1876, and there wasn't a coin in his pocket dated any later."

Captain Rihm looked at me questioningly. "Well,"

I said, glancing up from my notebook, "that could happen."

"Sure, it could," he answered in a satisfied tone, "but all the pennies he had were Indian-head pennies. Now, when did you see one of them last? There was even a silver three-cent piece; looked like an old-style dime, only smaller. And the bills in his wallet, every one of them, were old-time bills, the big kind."

Captain Rihm leaned forward and spat on the path, a needle-jet of tobacco juice, and an expression of a policeman's annoyed contempt for anything deviating from an orderly norm.

"Over seventy bucks in cash, and not a Federal reserve note in the lot. There were two yellow-back tens. Remember them? They were payable in gold. The rest were old national-bank notes; you remember them, too. Issued direct by local banks, personally signed by the bank president; that kind used to be counterfeited a lot.

"Well," Captain Rihm continued, leaning back on the bench and crossing his knees, "there was a bill in his pocket from a livery stable on Lexington Avenue: three dollars for feeding and stabling his horse and washing a carriage. There was a brass slug in his pocket good for a five-cent beer at some saloon. There was a letter postmarked Philadelphia, June, 1876, with an old-style two-cent stamp; and a bunch of cards in his wallet. The cards had his name and address on them, and so did the letter."

"Oh," I said, a little surprised, "you identified him right away, then?"

"Sure. Rudolph Fentz, some address on Fifth Avenue—I forget the exact number—in New York City. No problem at all." Captain Rihm leaned forward and spat again. "Only that address wasn't a residence. It's a store, and it has been for years, and nobody there ever

heard of any Rudolph Fentz, and there's no such name
in the phone book, either. Nobody ever called or made
any inquiries about the guy, and Washington didn't
have his prints. There was a tailor's name in his coat,
a lower Broadway address, but nobody there ever heard
of this tailor."

"What was so strange about his clothes?"

The Captain said, "Well, did you ever know anyone who wore a pair of pants with big black-and-white
checks, cut very narrow, no cuffs, and pressed without
a crease?"

I had to think for a moment. "Yes," I said then, "my
father, when he was a very young man, before he was
married; I've seen old photographs."

"Sure," said Captain Rihm, "and he probably wore
a short sort of cutaway coat with two cloth-covered
buttons at the back, a vest with lapels, a tall silk hat,
and a big, black oversize bow tie on a turned-up stiff
collar, and button shoes."

"That's how this man was dressed?"

"Like eighty years ago! And him no more than thirty
years old. There was a label in his hat, a Twenty-third
Street hat store that went out of business around the
turn of the century. Now, what do you make out of a
thing like that?"

"Well," I said carefully, "there's nothing much you
can make of it. Apparently someone went to a lot of
trouble to dress up in an antique style; the coins and
bills, I assume he could buy at a coin dealer's; and
then he got himself killed in a traffic accident."

"Got himself killed is right. Eleven fifteen at night
in Times Square—the theaters letting out; busiest
time and place in the world—and this guy shows up in
the middle of the street, gawking and looking around
at the cars and up at the signs like he'd never seen
them before. The cop on duty noticed him, so you can

see how he must have been acting. The lights change, the traffic starts up, with him in the middle of the street, and instead of waiting, the damned fool, he turns and tries to make it back to the sidewalk. A cab got him and he was dead when he hit."

For a moment Captain Rihm sat chewing his tobacco and staring angrily at a young woman pushing a baby carriage, though I'm sure he didn't see her. The young mother looked at him in surprise as she passed, and the captain continued:

"Nothing you can make out of a thing like that. We found out nothing. I started checking through our file of old phone books, just as routine, but without much hope because they only go back so far. But in the 1939 summer edition I found a Rudolph Fentz, Jr., somewhere on East Fifty-second Street. He'd moved away in 'forty-two, though, the building super told me, and was a man in his sixties besides, retired from business; used to work in a bank a few blocks away, the super thought. I found the bank where he'd worked, and they told me he'd retired in 'forty, and had been dead for five years; his widow was living in Florida with a sister.

"I wrote to the widow, but there was only one thing she could tell us, and that was no good. I never even reported it, not officially, anyway. Her husband's father had disappeared when her husband was a boy maybe two years old. He went out for a walk around ten one night—his wife thought cigar smoke smelled up the curtains, so he used to take a little stroll before he went to bed, and smoke a cigar—and he didn't came back, and was never seen or heard of again. The family spent a good deal of money trying to locate him, but they never did. This was in the middle eighteen seventies sometime; the old lady wasn't sure of the exact date. Her husband hadn't ever said too much about it.

"And that's all," said Captain Rihm. "Once I put in

one of my afternoons off hunting through a bunch of
old police records. And I finally found the Missing
Persons file for 1876, and Rudolph Fentz was listed, all
right. There wasn't much of a description, and no
fingerprints, of course. I'd give a year of my life, even
now, and maybe sleep better nights, if they'd had his
fingerprints. He was listed as twenty-nine years old,
wearing full muttonchop whiskers, a tall silk hat, dark
coat and checked pants. That's about all it said. Didn't
say what kind of tie or vest or if his shoes were the
button kind. His name was Rudolph Fentz and he
lived at this address on Fifth Avenue; it must have
been a residence then. Final disposition of case: not
located.

"Now, I hate that case," Captain Rihm said quietly.
"I hate it and I wish I'd never heard of it. What do
you think?" he demanded suddenly, angrily. "You
think this guy walked off into thin air in eighteen
seventy-six, and showed up again in nineteen fifty-five!"

I shrugged noncommittally, and the captain took it
to mean no. "No, of course not," he said. "Of *course*
not, but—give me some other explanation."

I could go on. I could give you several hundred such
cases. A sixteen-year-old girl walked out of her bedroom one morning, carrying her clothes in her hand
because they were too big for her, and she was quite obviously eleven years old again. And there are other occurrences too horrible for print. All of them have happened in the New York City area alone, all within the
last few years; and I suspect thousands more have occurred, and are occurring, all over the world. I could
go on, but the point is this: What is happening and
why? I believe that I know.

Haven't you noticed, too, on the part of nearly
everyone you know, a growing rebellion against the
present? And an increasing longing for the past? I

have. Never before in all my long life have I heard so many people wish that they lived "at the turn of the century," or "when life was simpler," or "worth living," or "when you could bring children into the world and count on the future," or simply "in the good old days." People didn't talk that way when I was young! The present was a glorious time! But they talk that way now.

For the first time in man's history, man is desperate to escape the present. Our newsstands are jammed with escape literature, the very name of which is significant. Entire magazines are devoted to fantastic stories of escape—to other times, past and future, to other worlds and planets—escape to anywhere but here and now. Even our larger magazines, book publishers and Hollywood are beginning to meet the rising demand for this kind of escape. Yes, there is a craving in the world like a thirst, a terrible mass pressure that you can almost feel, of millions of minds struggling against the barriers of time. I am utterly convinced that this terrible mass pressure of millions of minds is already, slightly but definitely, affecting time itself. In the moments when this happens—when the almost universal longing to escape is greatest—my incidents occur. Man is disturbing the clock of time, and I am afraid it will break. When it does, I leave to your imagination the last few hours of madness that will be left to us; all the countless moments that now make up our lives suddenly ripped apart and chaotically tangled in time.

Well, I have lived most of my life; I can be robbed of only a few more years. But it seems too bad—this universal craving to escape what could be a rich, productive, happy world. We live on a planet well able to provide a decent life for every soul on it, which is all ninety-nine of a hundred human beings ask. Why in the world can't we have it?"

COUSIN LEN'S WONDERFUL
ADJECTIVE CELLAR

Cousin Len found his wonderful adjective cellar in a pawnshop. He haunts dusty Second Avenue pawnshops because they're such a relief, he says, from Nature. Cousin Len doesn't like Nature very much. He spends most of his days outdoors gathering material for "The Lure and Lore of the Woods," which he writes, and he would rather, he says, be a plumber.

So he tours the pawnshops in his spare time, bringing home stereoscopic sets (World's Fair views, Chicago, 1893), watches that strike the hours, and china horses which hold toothpicks in their mouths. We admire these things very much, my wife and I. We've been living with Cousin Len since I got out of the Army, waiting to find a place of our own.

So we admired the adjective cellar, too. It had the grace of line of a fire hydrant, but was slightly smaller and made of pewter. We thought it was a salt cellar, and so did Cousin Len. He discovered it was really an adjective cellar when he was working on his column one day after he bought it.

"The jewel-bedecked branches of the faery forest are funereally silent," he had written. "The icy, steel-like grip of winter has stilled their summ'ry, verdant murmur. And the silv'ry, flutelike notes of its myriad, rainbow-dipped birds are gone."

At this point, naturally, he rested. And began to examine his saltcellar. He studied the bottom for the maker's mark, turning it in his hands, the cap an inch from his paper. And presently he saw that his manuscript had changed.

"The branches of the forest are silent," he read. "The grip of winter has stilled their murmur. And the notes of its birds are gone."

Now, Cousin Len is no fool, and he knows an improvement when he sees it. He went back to work, writing as he always did, but he made his column twice as long. And then he applied the adjective cellar, moving it back and forth like a magnet, scanning each line. And the adjectives and adverbs just whisked off the page, with a faint hiss, like particles of lint into a vacuum cleaner. His column was exactly to length when he finished, and the most crisp, sharp writing you've ever seen. For the first time, Cousin Len saw, his column seemed to say something. Louisa, my wife, said it almost made you want to get out into the woods, but Cousin Len didn't think it was that good.

From then on, Cousin Len used his adjective cellar on every column, and he found through experiment that at an inch above the paper, it sucks up all adjectives, even the heaviest. At an inch and a half, just medium-weight adjectives; and at two inches, only those of three or four letters. By careful control, Cousin Len has been able to produce Nature columns whose readership has grown every day. "Best reading in the paper, next to the death notices," one old lady wrote him. What she means, Len explained to me, is that his column, which is printed next to the death notices, is the very best reading in the entire paper.

Cousin Len always waits till we're home before he empties the adjective cellar: we like to be on hand. It fills up once a week, and Cousin Len unscrews the top and, pounding the bottom like a catchup bottle, empties it out the window over Second Avenue. And there, caught in the breeze, the adjectives and adverbs float out over the street and sidewalk like a cloud of almost invisible confetti. They look somewhat like miniature alphabet-soup letters, strung together and made of the thinnest cellophane. You can't see them at all unless the light is just right, and most of them are colorless. Some of them are delicate pastels, though. "Very," for example, is a pale pink; "lush" is green, of course; and "indubitable" is a dirty gray. And there's one word, a favorite with Cousin Len when he's hating Nature the most, which resembles a snip of the bright red cellophane band from around the top of a cigarette package. This word can't be revealed in a book intended for family reading.

Most of the time the adjectives and adverbs simply drop into the gutters and street, and disappear like snowflakes when they touch the pavement. But occasionally, when we're lucky, they drop straight into a conversation.

Mrs. Gorman passed under our window one day with Mrs. Miller, coming from the delicatessen. And a little flurry of adjectives and adverbs blew right into the middle of what she was saying. "Prices, these halcyon days," she remarked, "are evanescent, transcendental, and simply terrible. Mark my maniacal words, things are going straight and pre-eminently to the coruscated, indomitable, allegorical dogs."

Mrs. Gorman was pretty surprised, of course, but she carried it off beautifully, smiling grandly and patronizingly at Mrs. Miller. She has always contended that her ancestors were kings; now she claims they were also poets.

I suggested to Cousin Len, one time, that he save his adjectives, pack them into neatly labeled jars or cans, and sell them to the advertising agencies. Len pointed out, however, that we could never in a lifetime supply them in the quantities needed. We did, though, save up several shoe boxes full which we took along on a sight-seeing trip to Washington. And there, in the visitors' gallery over the Senate, we cautiously emptied them into a huge electric fan which blew over the floor. They spread out in a great cloud and drifted down right through a tremendous debate. Something must have gone wrong this time, though, for things didn't sound one bit different.

We're still using the wonderful adjective cellar, and Cousin Len's columns are getting better every day. A collection of them appeared in book form recently, which you've probably read. And there's talk of selling the movie rights. We also find Cousin Len's adjective cellar helpful in composing telegrams, and I used it, mostly at the inch-and-a-half level, in writing this. Which is why it's so short, of course.

OF MISSING PERSONS

Walk in as though it were an ordinary travel bureau, the stranger I'd met at a bar had told me. Ask a few ordinary questions—about a trip you're planning, a vacation, anything like that. Then hint about The Folder a little, but whatever you do, don't mention it directly; wait till he brings it up himself. And if he doesn't, you might as well forget it. If you can. Because you'll never see it; you're not the type, that's all. And if you ask about it, he'll just look at you as though he doesn't know what you're talking about.

I rehearsed it all in my mind, over and over, but what seems possible at night over a beer isn't easy to believe on a raw, rainy day, and I felt like a fool, searching the store fronts for the street number I'd memorized. It was noon hour, West 42nd Street, New York, rainy and windy; and like half the men around me, I walked with a hand on my hatbrim, wearing an old trench coat, head bent into the slanting rain, and the world was real and drab, and this was hopeless.

Anyway, I couldn't help thinking, who am I to see The Folder, even if there is one? Name? I said to myself, as though I were already being asked. It's Charley Ewell, and I'm a young guy who works in a bank; a teller. I don't like the job; I don't make much money, and I never will. I've lived in New York for over three years and haven't many friends. What the hell, there's really nothing to say—I see more movies than I want to, read too many books, and I'm sick of meals alone in restaurants. I have ordinary abilities, looks and thoughts. Does that suit you; do I qualify?

Now I spotted it, the address in the two-hundred block, an old, pseudo-modernized office building, tired, outdated, refusing to admit it but unable to hide it. New York is full of them west of Fifth.

I pushed through the brass-framed glass doors into the tiny lobby, paved with freshly mopped, permanently dirty tile. The green-painted walls were lumpy from old plaster repairs; in a chrome frame hung a little wall directory—white celluloid easily-changed letters on a black felt background. There were some twenty-odd names, and I found "Acme Travel Bureau" second on the list, between "A-1 Mimeo" and "Ajax Magic Supplies." I pressed the bell beside the old-style open-grille elevator door; it rang high up in the shaft. There was a long pause, then a thump, and the heavy chains began rattling slowly down toward me, and I almost turned and left—this was insane.

But upstairs the Acme office had divorced itself from the atmosphere of the building. I pushed open the pebble-glass door, walked in, and the big square room

was bright and clean, fluorescent-lighted. Beside the
wide double windows, behind a counter, stood a tall,
gray-haired, grave-looking man, a telephone at his
ear. He glanced up, nodded to beckon me in, and I
felt my heart pumping—he fitted the description exactly. "Yes, United Air Lines," he was saying into the
phone. "Flight"—he glanced at a paper on the glass-
topped counter—"seven-o-three, and I suggest you check
in forty minutes early."

Standing before him now, I waited, leaning on the
counter, glancing around; he was the man, all right,
and yet this was just an ordinary travel agency: big
bright posters on the walls, metal floor racks full of
folders, printed schedules under the glass on the
counter. This is just what it looks like and nothing
else, I thought, and again I felt like a fool.

"Can I help you?" Behind the counter the tall gray-
haired man was smiling at me, replacing the phone,
and suddenly I was terribly nervous.

"Yes." I stalled for time, unbuttoning my raincoat.
Then I looked up at him again and said, "I'd like to—
get away." You fool, that's too fast! I told myself. Don't
rush it! I watched in a kind of panic to see what effect
my answer had had, but he didn't flick an eyelash.

"Well, there are a lot of places to go," he said
politely. From under the counter he brought out a
long, slim folder and laid it on the glass, turning it
right side up for me. "Fly to Buenos Aires—Another
World!" it said in a double row of pale green letters
across the top.

I looked at it long enough to be polite. It showed
a big silvery plane banking over a harbor at night, a
moon shining on the water, mountains in the background. Then I just shook my head; I was afraid to
talk, afraid I'd say the wrong thing.

"Something quieter, maybe?" He brought out another folder: thick old tree trunks, rising way up out of sight, sunbeams slanting through them—"The Virgin Forests of Maine, via Boston and Maine Railroad." "Or"—he laid a third folder on the glass—"Bermuda is nice just now." This one said, "Bermuda, Old World in the New."

I decided to risk it. "No," I said, and shook my head. "What I'm really looking for is a permanent place. A new place to live and settle down in." I stared directly into his eyes. "For the rest of my life." Then my nerve failed me, and I tried to think of a way to backtrack.

But he only smiled pleasantly and said, "I don't know why we can't advise you on that." He leaned forward on the counter, resting on his forearms, hands clasped; he had all the time in the world for me, his posture conveyed. "What are you looking for; what do you want?"

I held my breath, then said it. "Escape."

"From what?"

"Well—" Now I hesitated; I'd never put it into words before. "From New York, I'd say. And cities in general. From worry. And fear. And the things I read in my newspapers. From loneliness." And then I couldn't stop, though I knew I was talking too much, the words spilling out. "From never doing what I really want to do or having much fun. From selling my days just to stay alive. From life itself—the way it is today, at least." I looked straight at him and said softly, "From the world."

Now he was frankly staring, his eyes studying my face intently with no pretense of doing anything else, and I knew that in a moment he'd shake his head and say, "Mister, you better get to a doctor." But he didn't. He continued to stare, his eyes examining my forehead now. He was a big man, his gray hair crisp and curling, his lined face very intelligent, very kind; he looked the way ministers should look; he looked the way all fathers should look.

He lowered his gaze to look into my eyes and beyond them; he studied my mouth, my chin, the line of my jaw, and I had the sudden conviction that without any difficulty he was learning a great deal about me, more than I knew myself. Suddenly he smiled and placed both elbows on the counter, one hand grasping the other fist and gently massaging it. "Do you like people? Tell the truth, because I'll know if you aren't."

"Yes. It isn't easy for me to relax though, and be myself, and make friends."

He nodded gravely, accepting that. "Would you say you're a reasonably decent kind of man?"

"I guess so; I think so." I shrugged.

"Why?"

I smiled wryly; this was hard to answer. "Well—at least when I'm not, I'm usually sorry about it."

He grinned at that, and considered it for a moment or so. Then he smiled—deprecatingly, as though he were about to tell a little joke that wasn't too good. "You know," he said casually, "we occasionally get people in here who seem to be looking for pretty much what you are. So just as a sort of little joke—"

I couldn't breathe. This was what I'd been told he would say if he thought I might do.

"—we've worked up a little folder. We've even had it printed. Simply for our own amusement, you understand. And for occasional clients like you. So I'll have to ask you to look at it here if you're interested. It's not the sort of thing we'd care to have generally known."

I could barely whisper, "I'm interested."

He fumbled under the counter, then brought out a long thin folder, the same size and shape as the others, and slid it over the glass toward me.

I looked at it, pulling it closer with a finger tip, almost afraid to touch it. The cover was dark blue, the shade of a night sky, and across the top in white letters it said, "Visit Enchanting Verna!" The blue cover was sprinkled with white dots—stars—and in the lower left corner was a globe, the world, half surrounded by clouds. At the upper right, just under the word "Verna," was a star larger and brighter than the others; rays shot out from it, like those from a star on a Christmas card. Across the bottom of the cover it said, "Romantic Verna, where life is the way it *should* be." There was a little arrow beside the legend, meaning Turn the page.

I turned, and the folder was like most travel folders inside—there were pictures and text, only these were about "Verna" instead of Paris, or Rome, or the Bahamas. And it was beautifully printed; the pictures looked real. What I mean is, you've seen color stereopticon pictures? Well, that's what these were like, only better, far better. In one picture you could see dew glistening on grass, and it looked wet. In another, a tree trunk seemed to curve out of the page, in perfect detail, and it was a shock to touch it and feel smooth paper instead of the rough actuality of bark. Miniature human faces, in a third picture, seemed about to speak, the lips moist and alive, the eyeballs shining, the actual texture of skin right there on paper; and it seemed impossible, as you stared, that the people wouldn't move and speak.

I studied a large picture spreading across the upper half of two open pages. It seemed to have been taken from the top of a hill; you saw the land dropping away at your feet far down into a valley, then rising up again, way over on the other side. The slopes of both hills were covered with forest, and the color was beautiful, perfect; there were miles of green, majestic trees, and you knew as you looked that this forest was virgin, almost untouched. Curving through the floor of the valley, far below, ran a stream, blue from the sky in most places; here and there, where the current broke around massive boulders, the water was foaming white; and again it seemed that if you'd only look closely enough you'd be certain to see that stream move and shine in the sun. In clearings beside the stream there were shake-roofed cabins, some of logs, some of brick or adobe. The caption under the picture simply said, "The Colony."

"Fun fooling around with a thing like that," the man behind the counter murmured, nodding at the folder in my hands. "Relieves the monotony. Attractive-looking place, isn't it?"

I could only nod dumbly, lowering my eyes to the picture again because that picture told you even more than just what you saw. I don't know how you knew this, but you realized, staring at that forest-covered valley, that this was very much the way America once looked when it was new. And you knew this was only a part of a whole land of unspoiled, unharmed forests, where every stream ran pure; you were seeing what people, the last of them dead over a century ago, had once looked at in Kentucky and Wisconsin and the old Northwest. And you knew that if you could breath in that air you'd feel it flow into your lungs sweeter than it's been anywhere on earth for a hundred and fifty years.

Under that picture was another, of six or eight people on a beach—the shore of a lake, maybe, or the river in the picture above. Two children were squatting on their haunches, dabbling in the water's edge, and in the foreground a half circle of adults were sitting, kneeling, or squatting in comfortable balance on the yellow sand. They were talking, several were smoking, and most of them held half-filled coffee cups; the sun was bright, you knew the air was balmy and that it was morning, just after breakfast. They were smiling, one woman talking, the others listening. One man had half risen from his squatting position to skip a stone out onto the surface of the water.

You knew this: that they were spending twenty minutes or so down on that beach after breakfast before going to work, and you knew they were friends and that they did this every day. You knew—I tell you, you *knew*—that they liked their work, all of them, whatever it was; that there was no forced hurry or pressure about it. And that—well, that's all, I guess; you just knew that every day after breakfast these families spent a leisurely half hour sitting and talking, there in the morning sun, down on that wonderful beach.

I'd never seen anything like their faces before. They were ordinary enough in looks, the people in that picture—pleasant, more or less familiar types. Some were young, in their twenties; others were in their thirties; one man and woman seemed around fifty. But the faces of the youngest couple were completely unlined, and it occurred to me then that they had been born there, and that it was a place where no one worried or was ever afraid. The others, the older ones, there were lines in their foreheads, grooves around their mouths, but you felt that the lines were no longer deepening, that they were healed and untroubled scars. And in the faces of the oldest couple was a look of—I'd say it was a look of permanent *relief*. Not one of those faces bore a trace of malice; these people were *happy*. But even more than that, you knew they'd *been* happy, day after day after day for a long, long time, and that they always would be, and they knew it.

I wanted to join them. The most desperate longing roared up in me from the bottom of my soul to *be* there—on that beach, after breakfast, with those people in the sunny morning—and I could hardly stand it. I looked up at the man behind the counter and managed to smile. "This is—very interesting."

"Yes." He smiled back, then shook his head in amusement. "We've had customers so interested, so carried away, that they didn't want to talk about anything else." He laughed. "They actually wanted to know rates, details, everything."

I nodded to show I understood and agreed with them. "And I suppose you've worked out a whole story to go with this?" I glanced at the folder in my hands.

"Oh, yes. What would you like to know?"

"These people," I said softly, and touched the picture of the group on the beach. "What do they do?"

"They work; everyone does." He took a pipe from his pocket. "They simply live their lives doing what they like. Some study. We have, according to our little story," he added, and smiled, "a very fine library. Some of our people farm, some write, some make things with their hands. Most of them raise children, and—well, they work at whatever it is they really want to do."

"And if there isn't anything they really want to do?"

He shook his head. "There is always something, for everyone, that he really wants to do. It's just that here there is so rarely time to find out what it is." He brought out a tobacco pouch and, leaning on the counter, began filling his pipe, his eyes level with mine, looking at me gravely. "Life is simple there, and it's serene. In some ways, the good ways, it's like the early pioneering communities here in your country, but without the drudgery that killed people young. There is electricity. There are washing machines, vacuum cleaners, plumbing, modern bathrooms, and modern medicine, very modern. But there are no radios, television, telephones, or automobiles. Distances are small, and people live and work in small communities. They raise or make most of the things they use. Every man builds his own house, with all the help he needs from his neighbors. Their recreation is their own, and there is a great deal of it, but there is no recreation for sale, nothing you buy a ticket to. They have dances, card parties, weddings, christenings, birthday celebrations, harvest parties. There are swimming and sports of all kinds. There is conversation, a lot of it, plenty of joking and laughter. There is a great deal of visiting and sharing of meals, and each day is well filled and well spent. There are no pressures, economic or social, and life holds few threats. Every man, woman and child is a happy person." After a moment he smiled. "I'm repeating the text, of course, in our little joke." He nodded at the folder.

"Of course," I murmured, and looked down at the folder again, turning a page. "Homes in The Colony," said a caption, and there, true and real, were a dozen or so pictures of the interiors of what must have been the cabins I'd seen in the first photograph, or others like them. There were living rooms, kitchens, dens, patios. Many of the homes seemed to be furnished in a kind of Early American style, except that it looked— authentic, as though those rocking chairs, cupboards, tables and hooked rugs had been made by the people themselves, taking their time and making them well and beautifully. Others of the interiors seemed modern in style; one showed a definite Oriental influence.

All of them had, plainly and unmistakably, one quality in common: You knew as you looked at them that these rooms were *home,* really home, to the people who lived in them. On the wall of one living room, over the stone fireplace, hung a hand-stitched motto; it said, "There Is No Place Like Home," but the words didn't seem quaint or amusing, they didn't seem old-fashioned, resurrected or copied from a past that was gone. They seemed real; they belonged; those words were nothing more or less than a simple expression of true feeling and fact.

"Who are you?" I lifted my head from the folder to stare into the man's eyes.

He lighted his pipe, taking his time, sucking the match flame down into the bowl, eyes glancing up at me. "It's in the text," he said then, "on the back page. We—that is to say, the people of Verna, the original inhabitants—are people like yourself. Verna is a planet of air, sun, land and sea, like this one. And of the same approximate temperature. So life evolved there, of course, just about as it has here, though rather earlier; and we are people like you. There are trivial anatomical differences, but nothing important. We read and enjoy your James Thurber, John Clayton, Rabelais, Allen Marple, Hemingway, Grimm, Mark Twain, Alan Nelson. We like your chocolate, which we didn't have, and a great deal of your music. And you'd like many of the things we have. Our thoughts, though, and the great aims and directions of our history and development have been—drastically different from yours." He smiled and blew out a puff of smoke. "Amusing fantasy, isn't it?"

"Yes," I knew I sounded abrupt, and I hadn't stopped to smile; the words were spilling out. "And where is Verna?"

"Light years away, by your measurements."

I was suddenly irritated, I didn't know why. "A little hard to get to, then, wouldn't it be?"

For a moment he looked at me; then he turned to the window beside him. "Come here," he said, and I walked around the counter to stand beside him. "There, off to the left"—he put a hand on my shoulder and pointed with his pipe stem—"are two apartment buildings, built back to back. The entrance to one is on Fifth Avenue, the entrance to the other on Sixth. See them? In the middle of the block; you can just see their roofs."

I nodded, and he said, "A man and his wife live on the fourteenth floor of one of those buildings. A wall of their living room is the back wall of the building. They have friends on the fourteenth floor of the other building, and a wall of *their* living room is the back wall of *their* building. These two couples live, in other words, within two feet of one another, since the back building walls actually touch."

The big man smiled. "But when the Robinsons want to visit the Bradens, they walk from their living room to the front door. Then they walk down a long hall to the elevators. They ride fourteen floors down; then, in the street, they must walk around to the next block. And the city blocks there are long; in bad weather they have sometimes actually taken a cab. They walk into the other building, they go on through the lobby, ride up fourteen floors, walk down a hall, ring a bell, and are finally admitted into their friends' living room—only two feet from their own."

The big man turned back to the counter, and I walked around it to the other side again. "All I can tell you," he said then, "is that the way the Robinsons travel is like space travel, the actual physical crossing of those enormous distances." He shrugged. "But if they could only step through those two feet of wall without harming themselves or the wall—well, that is how we 'travel.' We don't cross space, we avoid it." He smiled. "Draw a breath here—and exhale it on Verna."

I said softly, "And that's how they arrived, isn't it?

The people in the picture. You took them there." He nodded, and I said. "Why?"

He shrugged. "If you saw a neighbor's house on fire, would you rescue his family if you could? As many as you could, at least?"

"Yes."

"Well—so would we."

"You think it's that bad, then? With us?"

"How does it look to you?"

I thought about the headlines in my morning paper, that morning and every morning. "Not so good."

He just nodded and said, "We can't take you all, can't even take very many. So we've been selecting a few."

"For how long?"

"A long time." He smiled. "One of us was a member of Lincoln's cabinet. But it was not until just before your First World War that we felt we could see what was coming; until then we'd been merely observers. We opened our first agency in Mexico City in nineteen thirteen. Now we have branches in every major city."

"Nineteen thirteen," I murmured, as something caught at my memory. "Mexico. Listen! Did—"

"Yes." He smiled, anticipating my question. "Ambrose Bierce joined us that year, or the next. He lived until nineteen thirty-one, a very old man, and wrote four more books, which we have." He turned back a page in the folder and pointed to a cabin in the first large photograph. "That was his home."

"And what about Judge Crater?"

"Crater?"

"Another famous disappearance; he was a New York judge who simply disappeared some years ago."

"I don't know. We had a judge, I remember, from New York City, some twenty-odd years ago, but I can't recall his name."

I leaned across the counter toward him, my face very close to his, and I nodded. "I like your little joke," I said. "I like it very much, more than I can possibly tell you." Very softly I added, "When does it stop being a joke?"

For a moment he studied me; then he spoke. "Now. If you want it to."

You've got to decide on the spot, the middle-aged man at the Lexington Avenue bar had told me, *because you'll never get another chance. I know; I've tried.* Now I stood there thinking; there were people I'd hate never to see again, and a girl I was just getting to know, and this was the world I'd been born in. Then I thought about leaving that room, going back to my job, then back to my room at night. And finally I thought of the deep green valley in the picture and the little yellow beach in the morning sun. "I'll go," I whispered. "If you'll have me."

He studied my face. "Be sure," he said sharply. "Be certain. We want no one there who won't be happy, and if you have any least doubt, we'd prefer that—"

"I'm sure," I said.

After a moment the gray-haired man slid open a drawer under the counter and brought out a little rectangle of yellow cardboard. One side was printed, and through the printing ran a band of light green; it looked like a railroad ticket to White Plains or somewhere. The printing said, "Good, when validated, for ONE TRIP TO VERNA. Nontransferable. One way only."

"Ah—how much?" I said, reaching for my wallet, wondering if he wanted me to pay.

He glanced at my hand on my hip pocket. "All you've got. Including your small change." He smiled. "You won't need it any more, and we can use your currency for operating expenses. Light bills, rent, and so on."

"I don't have much."

"That doesn't matter." From under the counter he brought out a heavy stamping machine, the kind you see in railroad ticket offices. "We once sold a ticket for thirty-seven hundred dollars. And we sold another just like it for six cents." He slid the ticket into the machine, struck the lever with his fist, then handed the ticket to me. On the back, now, was a freshly printed rectangle of purple ink, and within it the words, "Good this day only," followed by the date. I put two five-dollar bills, a one, and seventeen cents in change on the counter. "Take the ticket to the Acme Depot," the gray-haired man said, and, leaning across the counter, began giving me directions for getting there.

It's a tiny hole in the wall, the Acme Depot; you may have seen it—just a little store front on one of the narrow streets west of Broadway. On the window is painted, not very well, "Acme." Inside, the walls and ceiling, under layers of old paint, are covered with the kind of stamped tin you see in old buildings. There's a worn wooden counter and a few battered chrome and imitation red leather chairs. There are scores of places like the Acme Depot in that area—little theater-ticket agencies, obscure busline offices, employment agencies. You could pass this one a thousand times and never really see it; and if you live in New York, you probably have.

Behind the counter, when I arrived, stood a shirt-sleeved man, smoking a cigar stump and working on some papers; four or five people silently waited in the chairs. The man at the counter glanced up as I stepped in, looked down at my hand for my ticket, and when I showed it, nodded at the last vacant chair, and I sat down.

There was a girl beside me, hands folded on her purse. She was pleasant-looking, rather pretty; I thought she might have been a stenographer. Across the narrow little office sat a young Negro in work clothes, his wife beside him holding their little girl in her lap. And there was a man of around fifty, his face averted from the rest of us, staring out into the rain at passing pedestrians. He was expensively dressed and wore a gray Homburg; he could have been the vice-president of a large bank, I thought, and I wondered what his ticket had cost.

Maybe twenty minutes passed, the man behind the counter working on some papers; then a small battered old bus pulled up at the curb outside, and I heard the hand brake set. The bus was a shabby thing, bought third- or fourthhand and painted red and white over the old paint, the fenders lumpy from countless pounded-out dents, the tire treads worn almost smooth. On the side, in red letters, it said "Acme," and the driver wore a leather jacket and the kind of worn cloth cap that cab drivers wear. It was precisely the sort of obscure little bus you see around there, ridden always by shabby, tired, silent people, going no one knows where.

It took nearly two hours for the little bus to work south through the traffic, toward the tip of Manhattan, and we all sat, each wrapped in his own silence and thoughts, staring out the rain-spattered windows; the little girl was asleep. Through the streaking glass beside me I watched drenched people huddled at city bus stops, and saw them rap angrily on the closed doors of buses jammed to capacity, and saw the strained, harassed faces of the drivers. At Fourteenth Street I saw a speeding cab splash a sheet of street-dirty water on a man at the curb, and saw the man's mouth writhe as he cursed. Often our bus stood motionless, the traffic light red, as throngs flowed out into the street from the curb, threading their way around us and the other waiting cars. I saw hundreds of faces, and not once did I see anyone smile.

I dozed; then we were on a glistening black highway somewhere on Long Island. I slept again, and awakened in darkness as we jolted off the highway onto a muddy double-rut road, and I caught a glimpse of a farmhouse, the windows dark. Then the bus slowed, lurched once, and stopped. The hand brake set, the motor died, and we were parked beside what looked like a barn.

It *was* a barn. . . . The driver walked up to it, pulled the big sliding wood door open, its wheels creaking on the rusted old trolley overhead, and stood holding it open as we filed in. Then he released it, stepping inside with us, and the big door slid closed of its own weight. The barn was damp, old, the walls no longer plumb, and it smelled of cattle; there was nothing inside on the packed-dirt floor but a bench of unpainted pine, and the driver indicated it with the beam of a flashlight. "Sit here, please," he said quietly. "Get your tickets ready." Then he moved down the line, punching each of our tickets, and on the floor I caught a momentary glimpse, in the shifting beam of his light, of tiny mounds of countless more round bits of cardboard, like little drifts of yellow confetti. Then he was at the door again, sliding it open just enough to pass through, and for a moment we saw him silhouetted against the night sky. "Good luck," he said. "Just wait where you are." He released the door; it slid closed, snipping off the wavering beam of his flashlight; and a moment later we heard the motor start and the bus lumber away in low gear.

The dark barn was silent now, except for our breathing. Time ticked away, and I felt an urge, presently, to speak to whoever was next to me. But I didn't quite know what to say, and I began to feel embarrassed, a little foolish, and very aware that I was simply sitting in an old and deserted barn. The seconds passed, and I moved my feet restlessly; presently I realized that I was getting cold and chilled. Then suddenly I knew—and my face flushed in violent anger and a terrible shame. We'd been tricked! Bilked out of our money by our pathetic will to believe an absurd and fantastic fable and left, now, to sit there as long as we pleased, until we came to our senses finally, like countless others before us, and made our way home as best we could. It was suddenly impossible to understand or even remember how I could have been so gullible, and I was on my feet, stumbling through the dark across the uneven floor, with some notion of getting to a phone and the police. The big barn door was heavier than I'd thought, but I slid it back, took a running step through it, then turned to shout back to the others to come along.

You have seen how very much you can observe in the fractional instant of a lightning flash—an entire landscape sometimes, every detail etched on your memory, to be seen and studied in your mind for long moments afterward. As I turned back toward the open door the inside of that barn came alight. Through every wide crack of its walls and ceiling and through the big dust-coated windows in its side streamed the light of an intensely brilliant blue and sunny sky, and the air pulling into my lungs as I opened my mouth to shout was sweeter than any I had ever tasted in my life. Dimly, through a wide, dust-smeared window of that barn, I looked—for less than the blink of an eye—down into a deep majestic V of forest-covered slope, and I saw, tumbling through it, far below, a tiny stream, blue from the sky, and at that stream's edge between two low roofs a yellow patch of sun-drenched beach. And then, that picture engraved on my mind forever, the heavy door slid shut, my fingernails rasping along the splintery wood in a desperate effort to stop it—and I was standing alone in a cold and rain-swept night.

It took four or five seconds, no longer, fumbling at that door, to heave it open again. But it was four or five seconds too long. The barn was empty, dark. There was nothing inside but a worn pine bench—and, in the flicker of the lighted match in my hand, tiny drifts of what looked like damp confetti on the floor. As my mind had known even as my hands scratched at the outside of that door, there was no one inside now; and I knew where they were—knew they were walking, laughing aloud in a sudden wonderful and eager ecstasy, down into that forest-green valley, toward home.

I work in a bank, in a job I don't like; and I ride to and from it in the subway, reading the daily papers, the news they contain. I live in a rented room, and in the battered dresser under a pile of my folded handkerchiefs is a little rectangle of yellow cardboard. Printed on its face are the words, "Good, when validated, for one trip to Verna," and stamped on the back is a date. But the date is gone, long since, the ticket void, punched in a pattern of tiny holes.

I've been back to the Acme Travel Bureau. The first time the tall gray-haired man walked up to me and laid two five-dollar bills, a one, and seventeen cents in change before me. "You left this on the counter last time you were here," he said gravely. Looking me squarely in the eyes, he added bleakly, "I don't know why." Then some customers came in, he turned to greet them, and there was nothing for me to do but leave.

Walk in as though it were the ordinary agency it

seems—you can find it, somewhere, in any city you try! Ask a few ordinary questions—about a trip you're planning, a vacation, anything you like. Then hint about The Folder a little, but don't mention it directly. Give him time to size you up and offer it himself. And if he does, if you're the type, if you can believe—then make up your mind and stick to it! Because you won't ever get a second chance. I know, because I've tried. And tried. And tried.

SOMETHING IN A CLOUD

You'd never have looked twice at Charley if you'd seen him there, moving along through the crowds in Penn Station—neither did anyone else. No one looked even once, except a tiny girl who was holding her mother's hand and who smiled up at Charley in instant friendship and love as he passed. No one else even glanced at the little sailor, for he was small, undersized even, altogether insignificant.

But Charley didn't know that, and he moved along confidently, briskly, through the crowds in the winter gloom of the station. His white hat, held by hope or magic to the back of his head, was only five feet, five inches above the floor. Though Charley was aware of his height statistically, he felt somehow taller. He weighed three pounds less than Anita Eckberg, but in his mind he was stalwart. Only a happy little smile saved his thin, sharp face from downright homeliness, but he had never heard of an inferiority complex, and, most of the time, was unaware of the concept.

His experiences in the past nineteen years almost

invariably contradicted this habitual optimism; Charley glimpsed briefly the facts of life as they applied to small and insignificant men. But only briefly, temporarily, for Charley knew, from the far wider experience of life supplied by the movies, that romance was waiting for him, as for everyone else, just around the corner.

He turned this corner now, into a station passageway, and headed for a row of phone booths. He glanced at a slip of paper he held on which a name and phone number were written. In the booth he dialed carefully, his eyes on the paper lying on the shelf under the phone. Then his expression and posture altered. His thin body tensed and he leaned forward, shoving his cap to the front of his head at a cocky angle. His smile vanished, his eyes narrowed, one brow lifted jauntily, and these tiny muscle movements transmitted themselves to his brain as a picture. His face *felt*, somehow, that it looked very like a younger Ronald Colman playing Rudolf in "The Prisoner of Zenda." As he cleared his throat, ready to speak, the sound was surprisingly deep, resonant and confident.

The phone rang in a bedroom twenty-four blocks south of Penn station and four stories up. A girl, lying on the bed, jumped to answer the phone. She tossed aside her magazine, the cover of which pictured a disheveled young woman struggling with an ape, and her plain little face smiled eagerly. She moved rapidly, the tight little spikes of her hair, clenched in the teeth of aluminum jaws, vibrating like antennae as she moved. She was thin and small, very little over five feet high, weighing less than ninety-five pounds. The big, old bed sagged in the middle, and she had to struggle up the sides of its concave surface, and before she succeeded, the phone rang again.

Charley saw none of these things, of course. He

heard only the ringing sound of the phone, and he wet his lips and smiled hopefully.

The girl stood now, tightening the cord of her old brown bathrobe. As she walked toward the phone she moved slowly, allowing it to ring once again, and her negligible hips swayed slightly. She surveyed the room haughtily, her eyes passing over, though not really seeing, the battered wooden dresser, tiny wash-basin, dust-colored rug, or the wallpaper designed by a manic-depressive. Then she lifted the phone and spoke, and the voice that came from this plain and diminutive girl would have surprised—even astonished—Charley if he had been there to see her.

But he didn't see her and and was not astonished; only delighted. Kim Novak might have answered the phone in just that way, or Katherine Hepburn, or Greta Garbo. This was, in fact, a blend of the better qualities of all three of these voices. All she said was "Hello," but it was a low and vibrant liquid sound, the practiced essence of a thousand movies, rich, lovely and thrilling. This wonderful sound traveled uptown with the speed of light, emerging from the receiver at Charley's ear, and instantly a curious thing happened.

Above Charley's phone booth in Pennsylvania Station, a small gray cloud formed. It was a little vague in outline, its edges wispy, fleecy. From the bottom of this cloud a tail protruded, like a curved sword, a scimitar, down into the phone booth, ending in a sharp point just over Charley's head. As it formed, the interior of the cloud was illuminated by a soft pink light.

Strangely, no one in the station noticed this cloud; but then most of these hurrying people frowned down at the floor, and none of them lifted their eyes.

Inside this cloud, in full, rich color over Charley's

head, a girl lay on a chaise lounge. She wore a flame-colored evening dress and was very beautiful. Her hair, as soft as cobwebs, was canary gold; her eyes were blue and long-lashed; her lips a moist and living red; somehow her face was indistinct. Her figure was magnificent, straining in places at her brilliant gown, and she lay, one long leg outstretched, the other raised to reveal, through a slit in the skirt, a perfect half-sphere of nylon-skinned knee. She lay there in languorous grace, her lovely face tilted up to the white-enameled phone that she held casually, her loose sleeve trailing down her slim white arm.

"Hello?" said the astonishing voice in the receiver at Charley's ear, and the red lips of the girl in the cloud over his head formed the same word.

Charley replied, and if the girl's voice was astonishing, his was astounding. It was neither high-pitched nor did it squeak; it bore no relation, in fact, to the little sailor in the phone booth who used it. Ronald Coleman says hello in a very similar way; a nearly identical way, in fact, for Charley had practiced.

"Hello," Charley's wonderful voice replied in the receiver in the bedroom twenty-four blocks downtown, and instantly another cloud, very like his, formed in the air above the girl's head. It was a shade more shallow, however, a little more cramped, for the bedroom ceiling was rather low. In fact, as she stood there holding the phone, the girl's head nearly touched the bottom of the cloud, and the tallest spike of her hair protruded into its lower edge. From the side of the cloud a long tail shot out, curving back into a point aimed at the girl's left ear.

Within the cloud's luminous interior, a man appeared, cut off at the waist by the lower edge of the cloud, but seeming to be, in relation to the room in which he stood, just under six feet six inches tall. He might have used a yardstick as a hanger for his jacket, which fitted his shoulders to perfection. It was dark in color and seemed to be a dinner jacket, for the young man stood in profile, revealing a black bow tie and the front of an immaculate, starched white shirt. His nose was very straight, his chin strong and full, and his black hair, glossy at the sides, broke on top into crisp little waves. The young man in the fleecy cloud was leaning casually, negligently, on the white mantel of a great, open fireplace.

"This is Charles Blaine," said Charley's amazing voice from the phone in the girl's hand, and the lips of the man in the cloud over her head formed the same words, smiling a little, his white teeth flashing in the firelight. A lighted cigarette in a long ivory holder appeared suddenly in the left hand; he flicked the ashes delicately, gracefully, toward the open flames. "Is this," the resonant, cultured voice from the telephone continued, and then dropped, softly, caressingly, "Annie Beasely?"

"Yes," Annie replied with a Hepburn-Novak-Garbolike sigh, and with exquisite grammar, "this is she."

"Well," said the phone at her ear, "you don't know me, but"—then intimately, softly—"you will soon, I hope," and over her head, in the cramped cloud in Annie's little bedroom, a butler wearing a vest, striped horizontally in contrasting shades of green, crossed the book-lined wall at the back of the huge room in which the young man seemed to stand, and the young man turned his broad back nearly filling the cloud, in order to watch him.

"My ship just got in tonight," Charley's voice continued from the phone. "I'm in the Navy." The young man in the cloud over Annie's head turned lazily to face front. His bow tie had become a long, black, beautifully tied cravat, and his jacket was now dark blue. Over the left breast pocket was a double row of ribbons; his cigarette holder had become a pipe, and on each sleeve of his coat was a triple band of gold. His face was darker, tropically tanned, and he smiled intimately. "One of the men"—the voice in the phone subtly emphasized this last word—"one of the men suggested I call you. Do you remember Benny? Benny Aicher."

"Oh," said Annie, and she laughed, pleasantly, liquidly. "Dear Ben. How is Ben? I haven't heard from him in quite a long time."

"He's fine, just fine," Charley's wonderfully modulated voice replied, and the young officer overhead smiled with Annie in tolerant remembrance of dear Ben. "He's not with us this trip, but he thought maybe—perhaps that is—you'd come to dinner with me; I'm a stranger in New York."

Annie smiled eagerly, excitedly, and shuffled her feet nervously, stepping closer to the phone. But when she spoke, her voice seemed doubtful. "Well-l" she said slowly, "I don't know."

This lovely sound, with its doubt and hesitation, sped through the wires to Pennsylvania Station, was reproduced in the receiver at Charley's ear, and in the pink mist over his phone booth the gorgeous girl in red frowned slightly, thoughtfully. Then her lips moved as Annie's voice continued, "I'm not dressed."

Instantly, delightfully, the red gown disappeared from the cloud over Charley's phone booth, and the stunning girl lay there, one slim leg still outstretched on the chaise lounge, one lovely knee raised; she wore only a pink bra, incredibly sheer silk stockings, and a really enchanting, lace-edged half-slip. She was a beautiful creature.

He smiled happily, and for a moment his voice lost its Colmanesque quality and climbed one full and excited octave. "Well," he squeaked, "maybe I'd better come d—"

"But I think I can make it," said Annie hastily. "Now, let me see." The voice in Charley's ear paused for a moment, and the girl over his head leaned forward, riffled the pages of a leather-bound notebook on the table beside her, studied a page for a moment, then leaned back again and smiled sweetly. "Yes," said Annie, "I'm free tonight."

"Good," said Charley, "wonderful!" His voice in the phone at Annie's ear was again deep, rich, suave and gentle. "Should I—shall I—come down and pick you up?"

"No-o," she said thoughtfully, and glanced round her room. "It's too long a trip, and we'd just have to go uptown again. I'll meet you. Where are you, at your hotel?" In the soft pink mist over her head, a door opened and a waiter appeared carrying a large silver bucket from which the neck of a tall green bottle protruded. The young Commander at the phone gestured suavely, indicating a place on the floor, and the waiter put down the bucket and quietly left the hotel room.

"No," said Charley, "I'm in a phone booth. At Penn Station. I called the minute I got in." For a moment the cloud over Annie's head went dim, then it brightened and the young Commander sat in a phone booth, wearing, rakishly, a gold-braided cap.

"Well," said Annie, "I'll meet you there, at the station. Did you say Penn Station? I could meet you at the foot of the escalators."

"Fine," he said. " 'Bout a quarter to eight?"

"I'll try to make it," she said graciously; then suddenly her eyes widened and the antennalike spikes of bound-up hair stood even more rigidly erect. Her mouth opened slowly, and when she spoke again, all traces of Hepburn, Novak and Garbo were gone, replaced by the voice of stark reality. "But how will you *know* me?" she wailed.

The six-foot-six voice from the movies laughed gently, deliciously amused. "Oh," it said, "don't worry; I'll know *you* all right. See you soon." And then the voice ended in a caressing tone. " 'Bye."

"Well," said Annie doubtfully, and for a moment the naked facts of life stood staring her in the face; then they were smothered and lost in a fog of pink mist. "All right," said Katherine, Kim and Greta, and then, lingeringly, " 'Bye, now."

The young, handsome naval officer in the cloud over her head picked up his bag and strode jauntily off, returning the salute of an enlisted man, and disappeared in the dissolving mist.

In Penn Station, Charley stepped from the phone booth, hitched up his pants, adjusted his hat, tilting it sharply over one eye, and walked off, smiling blissfully while the girl in the cloud over the phone booth selected a bonbon from a box on the table, and stood, hands on her hips, surveying her figure approvingly; and then, swaying gracefully, walked away and faded out, humming "Toujours L'Amour."

At seventeen minutes of eight, by the great clocks suspended in the mighty entrance archways, Penn Station was busy. Under the tremendous ceiling, infinitely high over their heads, hundreds of tiny figures crisscrossed the vast marble acres of floor space. At the escalators, sluggishly flowing up to and down from the long corridor that led out to the street, a small knot of people moved and shifted, stepping onto or off the moving stairs. Others stood waiting, out of the way at the sides of the escalators, watching the faces of the moving crowd.

In one of these waiting groups stood Charley, his shoes newly shined, arms folded on the knotted black kerchief on his chest. His lips were puckered in a noiseless whistle, and he occasionally rocked back on his heels, then forward on his toes, his thin white face content and expectant.

On the other side of the escalators stood Annie, in her green cloth coat with the beaver collar. She wore her new black hat, and stood, feet together, hands folded demurely over her shiny patent-leather bag. Her small white face was now whiter still from powder, her lips were reddened, and her brown hair hung below her hat in stiff and regular waves. She stood there, small and sweet, very neat and very young. She looked hopeful, expectant, as she watched the people streaming by.

They waited quietly, Charley on one side of the moving stairs, Annie on the other, their heads turning slowly, searching the crowd. Once or twice they glanced up at the clocks, but leisurely, unworriedly, for it was still only sixteen minutes of eight. Occasionally their glances crossed, their eyes met for a moment, but impersonally, not stopping, and moved past and beyond each other, searching for someone who had not yet appeared and to whom the other bore no resemblance.

They waited quietly, serene and patient, and presently, very nearly at the same time, their eyes grew dreamy. Once again twin clouds formed over their heads. The clouds were oval in shape, smoke-white in color, their circumferences scalloped in neat arcs, and from the bottom of each a tail curved downward, narrowing into points over each of their heads.

The clouds had no depth, they were paper thin, and they almost met over the moving stairs. Occasionally the head of a more than usually tall man or woman, ascending or descending on the escalators, passed directly through the bottom edge of one of these clouds, but none of them seemed to notice. Nor did any of the hundreds of people on the vast floor of the station seem to see these neat clouds; except once, when an elderly man hurrying to the Long Island trains glanced up, narrowed his eyes in astonishment, then shook his head as though dismissing and denying what he had seen. And he simply clutched his newspaper more tightly under his arm, hurried on across the floor, and disappeared through the exit to the lower level.

Within the cloud over Charley's head was reproduced that section of the station floor immediately before him. And across it, too, there moved hurrying people. But in the cloud they were dim and ghostlike, except for one figure that stood out from the others in bold relief.

She might have been a model or a showgirl or the heiress to eight million dollars. She was slim and tall, her hair like cornsilk and the color of new gold. She moved with the grace of a dancer, her legs slim and lovely, and she wore an indistinct but exquisitely tailored black coat; over one arm she carried a vague but rich fur. She was wonderfully pretty, though her face, too, was somewhat unclear, and she seemed to be looking for someone. Below the cloud, his eyes half closed, rocking gently on his feet, heel to toe, Charley stood smiling complacently.

The girl in the cloud moved her head gracefully, her face prettily puzzled as she tried to peer around or— standing on tiptoe—over the heads of passers-by. Then suddenly she smiled and moved forward swiftly, both hands outstretched in greeting.

"Charley?" she seemed to say, in a soft flutelike tone. "Charles Blaine?" And in the cloud, a figure stepped out to meet her,

He resembled, vaguely, the dreamy sailor who stood underneath the cloud. He, too, wore a sailor's uniform, but it fitted his slim strong body to perfection. His face, also, was thin—slim, rather—and he looked like Charley as a handsome brother resembles the ugly duckling of a family. Somehow, though the girl whose hands he now held was surely five feet six inches tall, the sailor in the cloud was taller still. Below this happy scene, on the station floor, Charley smiled dreamily.

The young naval officer, too, in the adjacent cloud over Annie's head, was hurrying across the station, his face eager and alert. Then he smiled and began to run gracefully forward, skillfully avoiding the drab ghosts around him. And below the long tail, which curved down from this cloud, Annie smiled a little, shyly; her eyes were discreetly lowered.

Abruptly, the scene in Charley's cloud disappeared, like a light snapped off, and the cloud itself began to sway and buckle, and to lose its sharp definition at the edges. Then it broke up, swiftly, into long trailing fragments that coiled and twisted like smoke, separating into smaller and smaller strands that swelled and thinned and dissolved in the air of the station. And Charley, his head thrust forward, his mouth slowly opening, stared at a girl weaving through the crowds in the distance, and moving, indisputably, toward the escalators at which he stood.

She was, if anything, even lovelier than the late occupant of Charley's cloud, and considerably more real. She was equally slim, graceful, beautifully dressed, and though she had no furs she carried a huge green purse as though it were ermine. She was not smiling, though, but frowning a little, moving her lovely head imperiously from side to side, impatiently trying to see through the crowd, and she was, definitely, moving toward the foot of the escalators, where Charley stood.

He was facing reality now, and as always he faced

it bravely. But somehow, as so often happened with
Charley, this real-life scene wasn't working out as well
as it might. For though he smiled and straightened to
his full five-feet-five, he saw that, undeniably, this approaching beauty was taller than he was. As he watched
her frowning in irritation at the crowd that impeded
her, it was just a little difficult to picture her standing
before him saying, "Charley? Charles Blaine?" and
smiling happily down at his face.

Nevertheless, Charley smiled in tentative greeting.
Though the message from his brain to the muscles of
his face requested a smile gay and debonair, it appeared
on his face a little weak and uncertain. He glanced
down at his blouse, which, plainly now, did not fit perfectly, and he nervously smoothed it with his hands.
His palms were suddenly moist, his tongue moved out
and wet his lips, he blinked his eyes, glanced down at
himself once more, and when he looked up now, the
smile was nearly gone and a look of doubt had sprung
into his eyes. Had he made a mistake in calling this
girl?

For a moment longer he stood, tremulously smiling,
facing this tall and haughty approaching beauty. Then
the last remnant of his smile went away, and onto his
face came the sickly look of a man who sees himself,
momentarily, as others see him.

For an instant the cloud reformed over his head, and
in it stood this girl with the green bag, her hands on
her hips, glaring wrathfully, incredulously, down at a
tiny, abject figure in a rumpled sailor suit. Then his
nerve broke and he stepped quickly to one side behind
a fat woman. Maybe the girl wouldn't notice him.

His eyes wincing in what he felt was contemptible
cowardice, his head turned away toward the escalators,
he stared miserably off into the distance, prepared to
deny that his name was Charles Blaine, though he

didn't think he'd be asked. And while his gaze passed directly through the space over Annie's head, his eyes did not see the few shattered tendrils of a white smoke-like substance there, which were writhing in agony and expanding into nothingness.

Nor did he see Annie's pale face, tense and frightened, staring off into the crowd at a young man, taller by several inches than most of the hurrying people through which he was making his way toward the escalators. The young man was no Commander, Lieutenant-Commander, or even a jaygee. There was no gold on his cap visor, but there was, on his sleeve, the lonely stripe of an Ensign; and he looked the way the voice in Annie's phone had sounded. He was indisputably handsome, clean-cut; he looked as though he might be a Yale man, and he seemed to be searching for someone. Annie nervously clenched her fists, rubbing the palms of her hands with her fingers. Then she averted her face. She could not help smiling a little in anticipation.

Several moments passed. Cautiously, Annie turned her head slightly to peer out at the station floor; then her head shot up and she turned to stare openly at the handsome, young Ensign, who stood now, smiling, the crowd dividing and flowing around them, holding both hands of a willowy blonde who held a large green purse under her arm.

Charley stared, too. He watched the tall, handsome young couple kiss—gaily, casually—watched them talk for a moment, then saw them turn and walk, her arm under his, into the crowd. He stood completely still, watching them disappear, his thin chest unmoving under his blouse. As they vanished, his chest heaved and he released his pent-up breath in an unhappy sigh of discouraged relief.

Some twenty feet away where Annie stood, this

sound, though lost in the hollow roar of Pennsylvania Station, was duplicated.

Now these two, the small, thin sailor and the tiny, thin girl, began to stroll, slowly, wearily, looking up at the clocks frequently and glancing worriedly, frowning at the faces of approaching people. For several moments they walked, sauntering aimlessly, glancing at the clocks again, turning and coming back to the escalators.

Then, in the midst of a step, Charley stopped dead still and his face puckered into an expression very close to horror, while above his head there appeared what seemed to be a puff of steam, then several more. These thickened, grew larger, and then, rapidly, like a movie in reverse, joined and formed a neat cloud again. But the tail, this time, appeared in the shape of a lightning bolt, the sharp point of which seemed to stab down into Charley's skull. Within the cloud, almost filling it like a movie close-up, a face appeared.

It seemed to be a female face; at least the dank, tangled hair above it was long. The face itself was round, pudgy and doughlike, the nose a fat blob, the eyes tiny and piglike, and it smiled—leered, rather—two jagged teeth protruding over the lower lip at each corner of the wide foolish mouth. "Charley?" it seemed to say, in an ugly rasp, "Charley Blaine?" and it grinned in gleeful, bestial welcome. Charley winced and shuddered, squeezing his eyes tight shut in horror.

Next to this gibbering, drooling monster, in a sickly white mist over Annie's head, stood a sailor four feet high with a face like a demented horse. He was, like earlier occupants of Annie's cloud, three feet wide, but in the hips, not the shoulders; he had no shoulders. Yellow flecks of egg clung to his pasty face next to the liverlike lips; above his eyes, so close they nearly merged, there were no eyebrows. There was no room for eyebrows, for his hair began immediately over the eyes, a thick mass of jutelike hair that ran up the narrowing sides of his head to the point that formed its top. Below this eager, maniacal figure, Annie stood cringing, her eyes on the floor, as she battled with nausea.

Then the twin clouds faded and disappeared, and the two figures below them opened their eyes, white-faced and shaken. Once again they began to pace, looking up at the clocks, and glancing at the faces of passers-by, but this time with stark apprehension.

They walked and they stood, they waited and watched, and presently, again, their eyes met and moved apart; but this time they became aware of each other. Their eyes swung back again, their gazes met, and now they held momentarily, then separated again. Charley and Annie both turned away. But almost at once their heads swung back, their eyes met once more, and this time they held the gaze.

Now Charley looked at the neat girl in the green cloth coat. She did not resemble even the least of the wonderful creatures who had moved through the clouds over his head, but on the other hand . . . Some of the fear and apprehension left his face. She was a good three inches shorter than Charley, and for the first time since he'd seen the girl with the big green purse, Charley's shoulders began to straighten. This girl was no model, she would never be a showgirl, but she was neat, Charley saw, she was young and fresh, and as he continued to watch her, the last remnants of horror faded from his face and his wilted spirit began to revive. With practically no justification at all, Charley began to feel rather stalwart again. He straightened his spine, cocked his hat to a jaunty angle, and smiled, he was pleasantly aware, not up but down at her face.

Annie-the-Dreamer looked at this sailor, but there was no pink mist over her head any more. Her eyes, still a little anxious and worried, were practical, realistic now. He was, she saw, no Commander, and there were no gold wings on his chest. But, on the other hand, he was alive, three-dimensional and real. He was here now, in the present, and he was smiling at *her*. And when he smiled, Annie noticed, his face was—rather nice. Annie smiled back and stepped forward toward him.

They greeted each other a little shyly, began to talk a little too rapidly, and each of them continued to study the other. Annie's voice was her own, now, with no trace of Hepburn, Novak, or Garbo. When they had confirmed their tentative recognition, she looked up at him, tossing her head a little defiantly, and said, "I bet you thought I'd look like Grace Kelly or somebody like that in the movies."

"Of course not," said Charley chivalrously, and his voice, too, now belonged to him. "I mean—of course not. You look fine. You look swell." He hesitated a moment, then added, *"You* prob'ly thought I'd be Marlon Brando or something."

"No," said Annie scornfully. "You look like I thought," and in a way she believed this now. "You look—cute," she said, and she smiled.

They talked for a time, chattering anxiously, laughing a good deal, and presently decided on a place for dinner, near Broadway and the movies, and turned to walk out of the station. As they did, the two clouds, for the last time, formed once more over their heads. The figure in Annie's cloud resembled Charley almost exactly, almost but not quite. As she looked up at Charley, the figure in her cloud grew a little; as she watched his face, smiling and laughing, the figure over her head, though still very like Charley, gradually became just a little more handsome. And it seemed a bit taller, more debonair.

While as Charley looked down at the smiling, animated face at his shoulder, he began to perceive its best features; the rather nice curve of her brows, the firm, young line of her chin. The figure in the mist over his head, though wearing Annie's green coat, became rather prettier, and presently, somehow, considerably more voluptuous. Charley was pleased with what he saw.

Arm in arm they walked toward the station exit, their faces turned to each other; overhead, the two clouds, trailing like captive balloons, bumped together, recoiling gently like colliding soap bubbles, then bumped once more, joining and merging into one. In this single, large cloud, the two figures, arm in arm now like the couple below, walked along, too, still resembling Annie and Charley in a way, but growing taller and more handsome, lovelier and more curvaceous, with every step. Presently the trailing cloud entered a puff of drifting smoke above a big, fat man smoking a cigar, and it did not emerge again.

On the sidewalk outside the station, they passed the young Ensign and the girl with the green purse stepping into a cab. Charley and Annie glanced at them briefly, but it was a look of mild interest only, a look of complete and friendly equality.

THERE IS A TIDE . . .

I'll say this for myself, and it's something that gripes me: if I had any other story to tell—if I said I'd seen a blue horse, a wild antelope or a three-toed sloth in my apartment—I'd finally be believed by the people who know me, when they saw I wasn't kidding, because I'm simply not the kind of guy to pull a pointless hoax. And I'm not a pathological liar.

I'm normal, I'm average, I even look like most people. I'm sound in body and limb, if not in wind; I'm married; twenty-eight years old; and I don't "imagine" or "dream" things that aren't so—a particularly exasperating explanation a number of people have offered me. I'll admit that at least once a week I imagine I'm president of McCreedy & Cluett, the big candy and cough-sirup company I work for, and once I even dreamed I was. But believe me, I don't sit down in the president's office and start giving orders. In the daytime, anyway, I have no trouble remembering that I'm actually assistant sales manager; no trouble distinguishing reality from what I imagine or dream.

The point I'm beating you over the head with is that, if I say I saw a ghost, people who know me ought to remember these things. I don't mind a few snickers at first; this sounds ridiculous, and I know it. In a modern, seventeen-story New York apartment building on East Sixty-eighth Street, I saw a plump, middle-aged ghost wearing rimless glasses. So snicker if you want, but at least consider the evidence before you laugh out loud.

I saw the ghost in my own living room, alone, between three and four in the morning, and I was there, wide awake, for a perfectly sound reason: I was worrying. The candy we make is doing pretty well, but the cough sirup isn't. It only sells by the carloads, that is, and the company would naturally prefer to measure sales in trainloads—big, long trains with two engines. That wasn't my problem as much as Ted Haymes's, the sales manager's. But I did see a chance in the whole situation, to put it bluntly, of beating him out of his job, and I worried about it, at the office, at home, at the movies, while kissing Louisa hello, good-by or what's new. Also while awake or asleep.

On this particular night, my conscience and I woke up around three, all set for some wrestling. I didn't want to disturb Louisa; so I grabbed the spare blanket and bundled up on the davenport in the living room. I did *not* sleep; I want to make that plain. I was full of my problem and wide awake. The street outside was dead; there'd be minutes at a time when not a car went by, and once, when a pedestrian passed, I could distinctly hear his footsteps three stories below. The room was dark, except for the windows outlined by the street lamp, and with no distractions, the battle of ambition versus conscience began. I reminded myself of the spectacular variety of ways in which Ted Haymes was a heel; you could hardly ask for a more deserving victim. Besides, I wouldn't be knifing him in the back, or anything.

I rationalized, I explained, I hunted for a way of talking myself into doing what I wanted to do, and maybe half an hour went by. I guess I'd been staring through the darkness down at the davenport, or the floor, or the cigarette in my hand, or something. Anyway, I happened to glance up, and there, clearly silhouetted against the street light, a man stood at the living-room windows with his back to me, staring down at the street.

My first quick thought was burglar or prowler, but in that same instant I knew it wasn't. His whole attitude and posture were wrong for it, because he simply stood there, motionless, staring down through the window. Oh, of course he moved a little; shifting his weight slightly, altering the position of his head a little. But in every way it was the attitude of a man up in the middle of the night over some problem.

Then he turned back into the room, and for an instant the street light caught his face from the side, and I saw it clearly. It was the face of a man around sixty; round, plump, undistinguished. He was quite bald and wore glasses, the eyes behind them wide in thought, and in that pale, harsh light I saw he was wearing a bathrobe, and I knew it was no prowler; I knew it was a ghost.

"How did you know?" some of my wiseacre friends have asked. "Was he transparent, yak, yak, yak?" No, he wasn't. "No long white sheet with holes for the eyes?" several dozen people with rare, rich senses of humor have asked. No, this figure moving in the faint light looked ordinary, harmless and real. And I knew it *wasn't,* that's all. I just knew.

"How did you feel?" people have asked, trying to keep their faces straight. I was terrified. The figure turned absently into the room and began to walk toward the hall leading to the bedroom and bathroom, and I could feel the thousands of separate little follicles on my head prickle and swell.

He did a strange thing. From the windows to the hall, the path is clear, yet he altered his direction for several steps, exactly as though he were walking around some piece of furniture that was no longer there.

And all up and down the middle of my back, the skin turned suddenly cold. I was horribly frightened, and I don't like the memory of it. Yet I wasn't worried. I felt no threat, that is, toward Louisa or me. I had the idea—the certainty, in fact—that for him I wasn't there at all, just as that invisible object *was* still there for him. And I knew, as he turned into the hall, out of my sight, that he wasn't going into the bedroom where Louisa lay, or into the bathroom, or anywhere else in that apartment. I knew he was going back into whatever time and place he had momentarily appeared from.

Our apartment is small, with just about adequate closet and cupboard space for a large family of mice. It took only a few minutes to search every last place a man might be hiding, and he was gone, as I'd known he would be. Some ghost, eh? A chubby, middle-aged ghost in a ratty old bathrobe; and not a moan, groan or peep out of him.

You know what occurred to me later, lying in bed wondering when I'd be able to sleep again? It just shows what silly thoughts you can have in the dark, especially when you've seen a ghost. He'd looked like a man who was fighting his conscience, and I suddenly wondered if it were the ghost of myself, half a lifetime later, still troubled by guilt, still talking myself into one more thing I knew I shouldn't do. My hair is thinning a little at the crown; I suppose I'll be bald someday. And if you added rimless glasses, forty pounds and thirty years . . . I was actually a little frightened, and, lying there in the darkness, I decided that next morning I was going to stop Ted Haymes from taking the step that would probably get me his job.

At breakfast, I couldn't quite bring myself to tell Louisa about my decision or what had happened; it was just too silly in the daylight. Louisa talked, though—about cough sirup and sales plans, promotions and more money, and bigger apartments, with a shrewd, intelligent, fur-coat look in her eyes. I mumbled some answers, feeling depressed. Then I put on my Homburg and left for the office, looking like a rising young executive and wishing I were dead.

Right after I got there, Ted strolled into my office and sat down on the corner of my desk, pushing my papers aside—a remarkably annoying and absolutely typical thing for him to do. He started yapping about his big new cough-sirup sales plan, of course; it was simple, direct, inexpensive and would sound good to the boss—I knew that. He had it all dressed up, but basically his play was distributing samples, in miniature bottles, during nice, brisk, pneumonia weather. He'd gotten cost figures, and he was about ready to present the plan and wanted to know if I agreed.

For a minute I just sat there, knowing his plan would flop, and him along with it. Then I just shrugged and said, yeah, I guessed he was ready. I was astonished; but at the same time I knew why I'd changed my mind. You've known someone like Ted if you ever worked in an office; they're standard equipment, like filing cabinets. He happens to be tall and skinny, though they come in all shapes, a bumptious sort of guy with a hideous, mocking horselaugh. He's a know-it-all, a pincher of stenographers, a credit hog—I've got to watch him all the time to see that I get any recognition for the work our department does—and even when he's patting you on the back, there's a sneer in his eyes.

Sitting at my desk after he'd left, I was perfectly willing again to give him the business. Then, unaccountably, the image of the ghost at my living-room windows flashed up in my mind. It made me suddenly furious—I didn't know why—and I knew I wanted that ghost explained and exorcised. Somehow I knew I had to get him out of my apartment and out of my mind.

Now, the building I live in is no ancient, crumbling castle with a history hopelessly shrouded in the mists of time. It was built in 1939 and is managed by Thomas L. Persons Company, a big realty firm. So I reached for the Manhattan telephone book, looked up their number and called them.

A girl answered in a brisk, bitter voice, and I explained that I was a rent-paying customer and wanted to know if she could tell me the names of previous tenants of my apartment. From the way she said, "Certainly not!" you'd thing I'd made an indecent proposal. I persisted, spoke to three more people and finally reached a man who grudgingly consented to open the archives and get me what I wanted.

A woman and her mother—no men in the family—had occupied my apartment from 1945 till 1954, when we moved in. In 1944, and for a few months after, the apartment's first tenants had lived there: a Mr. Harris L. Gruener—pronounced Greener—and his wife. The ghost was Gruener, I insisted to myself, and if it could possibly be done, I was going to prove that it was, and that it had nothing to do with me.

That night, around three, I woke up again, took the blanket from the foot of the bed and settled down on the davenport to settle Ted's hash. Deliberately I worked myself into a tough, ruthless frame of mind. "Business is business," I said to myself, lying there smoking in the dark. "All's fair, et cetera, and Ted Haymes would certainly do it to me, if the situation were reversed.

The nice thing was that I didn't actually have to *do* anything. I'd worked for a much smaller candy and cough-sirup company, before McCreedy & Cluett; and they had once tried what was virtually Ted's plan. It had looked good, sounded good—and it had failed completely. We figured out why. Except for the tiny fraction of people who happened to have coughs at the moment we gave out our samples, most of them dropped our little bottles into overcoat pockets, where they stayed for days. Presently they may have reached the shelves of medicine cabinets; and maybe eventually they were used, and even resulted in sales. But the immediate sales results of the plan were zero. And it was dropped, just as fast as we could let go.

I knew it would happen again. All I had to do was say nothing and look doubtful. When it failed, I'd be the man with the sales instinct who'd been pretty doubtful about the plan from the start, and—not right away, of course, but presently—I'd have Ted's job, and he'd be out. It wasn't sure-fire, but I had nothing to lose, and I lay there working out the best way of subtly getting my doubts on record with the boss.

Yet that wasn't all I was doing, and I knew it. It was the dead of night, utterly silent outside and in, and I knew I was also waiting for a ghost, and that I was actually afraid to light another cigarette.

And then the ghost came strolling in from the hall, his head down on his chest, wearing that mangy old bathrobe. He crossed the room to the windows, and then just stood there again, staring down at the street. For twenty minutes or so, he went through the same performance as he had the night before. I don't mean identically, every movement the same, like a movie you see twice. I had the feeling this was another night for him, and that he was up once again, standing at that window, working over the same old problem, whatever it was.

Then he left, just as before, walking around the invisible object that was no longer there, and I knew he was walking through another time.

I had to do something. I *knew* I had to prove to myself that this ghost had nothing to do with me, and I walked out to the hall telephone and, with my hands trembling, looked up Gruener in the telephone book. There were several listed, but, as I'd expected, no Harris L. Feeling relieved and a little silly now, I tried the Brooklyn directory—and there it was. *Harris L. Gruener,* it said in cold, black type, with a telephone number and address, and then I was really panicky. For it seemed certain that Gruener was nothing more than a previous tenant of this apartment, who now lived in Brooklyn, and had no connection with the ghost. And if the ghost wasn't Gruener . . . I wouldn't let myself think about that now, and I went to bed knowing where I had to go in the morning.

The house when I finally found it far out in Brooklyn, was a small white cottage; there was nothing unusual about it. A kid's bike and an old ball bat, split and wrapped with tape, were lying on the front porch. I pressed the button, and a musical chime sounded inside; then a woman in a house dress and apron came to the door. She was in her early thirties, I'd say; nice-looking but probably overworked. "Mr. Gruener?" I said.

She shook her head. "He's at work now." I'd half expected that and wished I'd telephoned first, but then she added, "Or do you mean his father?"

"Well," I said, "I'm not sure. I want Harris L. Mr. Harris L. Gruener."

"Oh," she answered, "he's around in the back yard." She smiled embarrassedly. "You mind walking around the side of the house? I'd ask you through, but it's in kind of a mess yet, and—"

"Of course not." I smiled understandingly, thanked her, touching my hat, then followed the walk around to the back yard. A moment or so later, fumbling with the latch of the rusted wire gate, I glanced up, and there in a garden lounge chair across the yard, face up to the sun, sat my Mr. Gruener.

It was a relief and at the same time a cold shock, an utterly frightening thing, and I just stood there, my hand still automatically fumbling with the gate, my mind churning to make sense out of this. I'd seen no ghost, I explained to myself; this man must be insane and had twice broken into my apartment in some unguessable way for some mad, secret reason. Then, as I got the gate open, Gruener opened his eyes, and I knew that I *had* seen a ghost.

For there, watching me approach, smiling pleasantly in greeting, was unquestionably the face I'd seen staring down at the street from my apartment window —but now it was a dozen years older. Now it was the face of a man in his seventies, looser, the muscle tone gone, the skin softer. With a courteous gesture of his hand, the old man invited me to take a chair beside him, and I sat down, knowing that what I'd seen in my apartment was this man—as he'd looked a decade before. Across the yard, his back against the board fence, a boy of perhaps twelve sat on the grass, watching us curiously, and for a moment I sat staring at him, trying to figure out what I could do or say. Then I turned to the old man and said, "I came because I've seen you before. In my apartment." Then I added my address and apartment number.

But he only nodded. "Used to live there," he agreed politely, and waited for me to go on. There was nothing else to do; I began at the beginning and told him what I'd seen. Gruener listened in silence, staring across the yard. I couldn't tell what he was thinking.

"Well," he said, smiling, when I finished, "it's all news to me. Didn't know there was a ghost of my former self wandering around 9 M. Don't tell the landlord, or they'll be charging one of us extra rent."

His voice broke on the last word. I looked at him closely, and his expression seemed to have collapsed. His mouth gaped; his eyes stared. Then—I was horrified—two tears squeezed out from the corners of his eyes, and he covered his face with his hands. "No, no, no," he moaned in a whisper, "oh, let me alone."

The old man sat there, his elbows on his knees, his face buried in his hands, breathing slowly and deeply, getting hold of himself. Presently, turning to face me, he sat erect again, dropping his hands, and the muscles of his face were controlled once more, and he stared at me, his eyes sick. "You're seeing something—I have no idea why—that I try every day of my life not to think of. I paced that apartment once. I stared out that window, just as you saw me." His face twisted, and he shook his head. "I can still see it—the way that street looked in the dead of night. Hateful, hateful."

For half a minute he sat, his eyes wide and staring; but he had to go on now—we both knew that—and I waited. Quietly, he said, "I was trying to make up my mind to kill myself." He glanced at me. "I wasn't despondent; nothing like that. It was simply and obviously the only possible conclusion to my life."

The old man sat back in his chair, his hands on the arms. "I was once nearly president of one of the largest investment firms in the world. I got there by hard work, as I often told people, and it was true. But I didn't say that I got there, also, on other men's backs. I was and am a selfish man; I knew it, and I was proud of it. Nothing and no one ever stood in the way of what I wanted, not my wife, or even my son—and he's paying for that now, and always will, though that's another story."

The old man reached out and tapped my arm with a curved forefinger. "I justified it, boy. If a man can't take care of himself, it is no one else's concern; I said that all my life, and practiced it. I became chief clerk of my firm, manager, junior vice-president, senior vice-president and had the presidency in my grasp, and what happened to those who stood in my way was their affair, not mine." He smiled sadly. "But I, too, stood in someone's way, I discovered; someone like me, only smarter still.

"And instead of the presidency, I was suddenly out

of the firm—out of a job and absolutely broke. By then, fortunately, I was a widower, but my home in the country was lost, and the rent was paid on the small apartment I used in the city during the week, for only nine more days, after which I had to move.

"In less than a single week's time, I was suddenly facing the choice of dependency, of actual charity or of ending my life; and the way I had lived demanded the latter. But I couldn't quite do it."

Contempt for himself was plain in his eyes as Gruener looked at me. "I almost could," he said. "I had it planned: sleeping tablets, with a note marked 'Private,' and mailed the evening before to an old friend, Dr. William Buhl. The note would have told Buhl what I'd done and why, and would have requested him to certify my death as heart failure. Whether he would have done so, I can't say; I could only have hoped that he would.

"Instead"—he spat the word out with sudden loathing—"I moved in here with my son and his family." He shrugged. "Oh, they were glad to have me, Lord knows why, though it meant extra expense, and they had to take the baby"—he nodded at the boy—"into their bedroom to make room for me.

"But if you think that's what bothered me, you're wrong. No, it was this: from a busy, prosperous man with considerable prestige in his occupation, I was suddenly turned into a nobody, living in a child's bedroom." He shook his head in disgust, and added, "Baby-sitting in the evenings, for the first six or eight years, helping with the dishes, reading the morning paper, listening to the radio in my bedroom with the Donald Duck wallpaper, sitting out here in the sun. That's been the absurd end to my life, just as I knew it would be when I made my decision."

Smiling bitterly, Gruener said, "And now you know

what I was pondering, staring down through the windows of apartment 9 M when somehow you saw me. I had the chance to justify the whole philosophy of my life—to be on top or forget the whole thing. But during two nights I could not achieve the courage to do it. And on the following night, I knew I had to. I stood there, I remember, staring down at that dismal street, hoping for help.

"Almost superstitiously, I stood hoping for some little sign, the least encouragement from somewhere or anywhere. That is all I needed, I am certain, to tip the balance in the right direction. But of course there was no sign; it was up to me alone. When the night began to end, I had to make my own decision, and you see what I chose." The old man stood up. "Why you should see my 'ghost' or whatever it was, I don't know." I stood, too, and we strolled toward the end of the yard. "But they say," he added, "that a particularly intense human experience can sometimes leave behind some sort of emanation or impression on the environment it happened in. And that under the right conditions it can be evoked again, almost like a recording that is left behind in the very air and walls of the room."

We reached the high wood fence and leaned on it, and Mr. Gruener turned to me, smiling a little. "Maybe that's what happened, boy. You, too, were up in the night in that very room. You, too, were pondering some problem, and maybe those were the right conditions: a sort of similarity of atmosphere that for a few moments could reach out and, like a delicate, beautifully tuned radio, bring back whatever impression my agonizing experience had made there. "Or," he said, losing interest, and turning back into the yard, "maybe somehow it brought back the actual time itself, twelve years before; I really don't know."

There was actually no comment to make, and all I could think of was, "Well, you made the right decision."

He stopped suddenly, there on the grass. "No, I did not! I've been a useless burden!" He walked on again, toward the chairs. "My son is no money-maker and never will be; he didn't even have a telephone when I came; so I had one installed, paying for it from the little income I still have. Pathetic, isn't it?" He smiled as we sat down. "Still trying to be somebody, even if no more than a name in a telephone book. Originally, I suppose, I had some idea that one of the firms would eventually be after me, in what capacity I don't know, and I wanted to be sure they could find me.

"No," he said belligerently, "I know now what I knew then: these extra years have meant nothing to me. And I also know now what I didn't even consider then: what these years have meant to my son, his wife and that child." He nodded at the boy across the yard. "I think he'd have a brother or sister now, if I could have done to myself what I did to others. As it is, there simply wasn't room for another baby, nor quite enough money. But without me, there would have been. I feel now what I would once have been incapable of feeling: that I deprived a grandchild of being born; a whole life was lost in exchange for something that should never have been—a few more useless years for me."

Quickly, anticipating my objections, he cut them off, ending the conversation. "Well," he said, nodding at the boy, "at least it's been good watching him grow and develop; he's a nice boy, and one of the few things I'm proud of."

It's obvious, of course—and was obvious to me on the way back to Manhattan, through the rest of that day at the office and all through that evening—that in a sense I *had* seen a ghost of my future self, there at

my apartment windows. Through the accident of oc-
cupying Gruener's apartment, I had somehow seen—
how or why I couldn't imagine—what I might become
myself.

But still, sitting and pretending to read that night,
while Louisa knitted, my problem was a long way from
the easy, obvious-at-a-glance dilemma of somebody else.
I sat remembering the faces of men in my office—and
they're in every office—who have reached their middle
thirties, with their big chance lost somewhere in the
past. At some point or another it dawns on them, and
from then on you can see it in their eyes, that the
confident ambition of their youth is never going to be
fulfilled.

Shakespeare said it; I remembered the quotation
vaguely, and got up and went to the bookshelves for
our one-volume complete Shakespeare, and finally
found the quotation in Julius Caesar. "There is a tide
in the affairs of men," Brutus says, "which, taken at
the flood, leads on to fortune; omitted, all the voyage
of their life is bound in shallows and in miseries. On
such a full sea are we now afloat; and we must take the
current when it serves or lose our ventures."

He was right, damn it! I sat there knowing it. You're
not handed a promotion for being a good boy, for
doing your work conscientiously, or for always getting
to the office on time! You're not handed it at all; you've
got to recognize the time for it and grab it while it's
there.

Of course I was awake again that night. I dragged
myself out to the davenport, and of course I saw
Gruener's ghost again; and this time I got mad. I
swear I hadn't even been thinking of him. I lay flat on
my back, staring at the ceiling, and for a long time I
was tempted to steer Ted Haymes off his idea, and kiss
my chance of stealing his job good-by. It was the peace

of mind waiting for me the instant I'd decided that tempted me; the good feeling I knew would come flooding over me. I wanted that, and I knew it would sustain me for days and weeks. But at the back of my mind lay the question: Then what? Two or three more years as assistant before, finally, past thirty, I somehow made sales manager? Just a little too late, a little too old to be a candidate still for the really important jobs at the top?

Lying there smoking in the dark, I *hated* Ted Haymes. He deserved nothing from me! The man was no good; was I going to sacrifice Louisa for *him*? I knew suddenly what was the matter with me. I was one of the timid people who want life to work out like a story, and when it doesn't, they retreat from it, and call their timidity virtue.

"There is a tide in the affairs of men," and this was mine and might never come again, and all of a sudden, in a flood of hot feeling, I was going to take it. I sat up on the davenport, shaken and deeply excited, knowing that from now on I was a different, tougher man, and I actually muttered out loud, giving myself a sort of miniature pep talk. "Do it!" I told myself. "Damn it, go ahead; all it takes is nerve." I felt pretty good, actually, and I started to get up, thinking I might even wake Louisa and tell her about it. And that's when I noticed Gruener's fat ghost in his crummy old bathrobe, standing at the windows again.

I was coldly furious; not scared in the least; and I really think I might have gone over to him and tried to do something about getting rid of him, though I don't know what. But he turned just then and once more crossed the room, avoiding the invisible barrier, and walked down the hall toward the bathroom, and then I remembered what Gruener had told me. He'd been up three nights with his problem, and now I'd seen him three nights, and I was certain this was the end of it. And it was. I went to bed then, and I've never seen Gruener's ghost since.

Have you ever noticed that once you decide you're going to give someone the business, you can't wait to start? And you can't lay it on too strong. Next morning at the office, I felt a kind of tough, hard cockiness about my decision, and I asked Ted to lunch. He's a wise guy, a sneerer, and I actually had a ghost story I could prove; undoubtedly I was the first man in history who had the ghost himself to back up his story, and Ted was the man I wanted to back out on a limb, and then break it off.

In the restaurant booth he listened, true to type, with an amused and pitying sneer on his face, and I wondered why I'd ever thought twice about giving him the least consideration. I didn't tell him, of course, what I'd actually been worrying over at night, but the rest was accurate, and occasionally, as I talked, he'd shake his head in mock pity—his idea of fine, rich humor. Then, when I finished, I let him sound off. I let him bray that mule laugh and listened patiently while he spouted theories about hallucinations, the ability of the mind to fool itself and the kind of glib psychiatric jargon people like Ted talk these days. He was the first of the many people who have assured me that I "dreamed" or "imagined" Gruener's ghost.

I let him rave, clear through dessert, knowing he was squirming to get back to the office and tell everybody, with a phony worried look, that I was "working too hard," and then wait for them to ask why. Finally, when he'd talked enough, I had him. I challenged him to go out to Gruener's with me that evening, and he had to say yes; he'd insulted me too much to say anything else. Then we just sat there, drinking coffee and stealing looks at each other.

People like Ted have a sort of low animal cunning, and pretty soon his eyes narrowed, and, excusing himself, he got up. A minute later he was back, beckoning slyly with his forefinger, like a stupid kid. He led me out to the telephone booth, and there, lying open at the G's, was a Brooklyn directory. "Show me," he said.

It wasn't there. The name Harris L. Gruener simply was not in the telephone book, that's all; and that afternoon at the office, people smiled when I went by, and once, when I was standing at the water cooler, someone called "Boo!" in a quavering, very comical voice. It might sound funny, but it drove me crazy—I *knew* what I'd seen—and a million dollars in cash couldn't have stopped me from doing what I did; I walked out of that office and headed for Brooklyn.

To my everlasting relief, the house was still there, looking just the same, and when I pushed the button, the musical chime sounded inside. No one answered; so I walked around at the side, and, sure enough, there was the rusty wire gate, and there was young Mrs. Gruener hanging out a wash. The boy was there, too, playing catch with another kid, and I felt so relieved I waved and called, "Hi!" very exuberantly.

Mrs. Gruener came over, and I said, "Hello." She answered grudgingly, the way housewives do when they're busy, as though I were a salesman or something. "Mr. Gruener home?" I said.

"No," she answered, "he's at work," and I wondered why we had to go through that routine again and wondered if she were stupid or something.

"No, I mean Mr. Gruener, Sr. Harris L., that is."

This time she really looked suspicious and didn't answer for several seconds. Then, watching my face, her voice flat, she said, "Mr. Gruener is dead."

She got her reaction; I was stunned. "When?" I managed to say. "I'm terribly sorry. When did it happen?"

Her eyes narrowed, hard as flint. "Who are you, mister? And what do you want?"

I didn't know what to say. "Don't you remember me?"

"No. Just what do you want, anyway?"

I could hardly think, but there was something I suddenly had to know. "I'm an old friend of his, and . . . didn't know he died. Tell me—please tell me—when did he die?"

In a cold, utterly antagonistic voice, she said, "He died twelve years ago, and all his 'old friends' knew it at the time."

I had to get out of there, but there was one more thing I had to say. "I could have sworn I'd seen him later than that. Right here, too; and you were here at the time. You're sure you don't remember me?"

She said, "I certainly am. Far as I know, I never saw you before in my life." She was telling the truth.

I've quit looking up Harris L. Gruener in Brooklyn telephone books, because the name is never there. But it was. It *was* there once, and I saw it; I didn't "dream" or "imagine" it, and all the Ted Haymeses in the world can't make me think so, and I'll tell you why! I phoned the doctor Gruener had mentioned. "Why, yes," he said—he sounded like a nice guy—"the cause of Gruener's death is public information; you could read it on the death certificate. Harris Gruener died of heart failure, twelve years ago."

I know it's not proof. I *know* that, but—don't you see? Out of the hundreds of cases that doctor must have treated in twelve years' time, *why did he remember this one instantly?* Unless there is something about it that will make it stick in his mind forever.

I know why. I know what happened. There in my living room, on that third night, knowing he had to make up his mind, Harris Gruener stood staring down

at the street. For him it was twelve years ago—1945—
and he stood waiting for a sign that would help him to
do what he felt he had to. For me, it was the present;
and as I lay there, a decision rose up in me, and I said
suddenly, intensely, "Do it! Damn it, go ahead; all it
takes is nerve." And across the years, across whatever
connection had been briefly evoked between us,
Gruener heard. He heard it, perhaps, as only a whisper,
or only in his mind.

But Gruener did hear it, I know, and more than
that, he understood what perhaps I did not—that,
morally, it was a decision for suicide. "Do it!" he
heard me say, and he of all people knew what that
meant, and—he did it. He turned then, I am certain,
back again in the year 1945, and he walked to the
bathroom where the sleeping tablets were. Then he
wrote a note to William Buhl, dropped it down the
hall mail chute and went to bed for the last time.

Don't ask me how it happened, or why—ask Einstein.
I don't know if time shifts sometimes; if events that
have already happened can be made to happen again,
this time in another way. I don't know *how* it could
happen; I only know that it did.

How do I know? That boy playing catch in the back
yard of the Gruener home was the same boy I saw the
first time, exactly. But the other boy, who was playing
catch with him; I didn't see him the first time, because
he wasn't there. He wasn't anywhere; he didn't exist.
But he does now, and I know who he is; there's no
mistaking the resemblance. He's the first boy's brother.
They're alike as twins, though not the same height;
the second boy is younger, by a year or so, I'd say.
They're nice kids; I'm certain of that. And I'm certain
that if old Mr. Gruener could see them, he'd be happy
and proud of his grandchildren—both of them.

No one really believes me, and I can't blame them,

I guess. Some people even think my story is a psychopathic excuse for failure; time is moving on and there's still an "Assistant" in front of my title. I wish I could say that Ted Haymes is grateful for that, and, while I doubt it, maybe he is. All morning, the day after I'd told him about Gruener's ghost, he'd amuse the whole office every chance he got by staring fatuously past my shoulder in horror as though he'd suddenly seen a ghost. With Ted, that kind of juvenile joke would ordinarily continue for weeks; but after I steered him off his sampling plan that afternoon, and explained why I had, he never pulled his joke again.

I doubt that it was from gratitude, but I do think he got a glimpse of the truth of what happened to me and was a little scared, for the same reason I was. And maybe from now on he'll be a little different sort of person, too; I really can't say.

But I'm grateful to Gruener, anyway. There in my living room he and I once stood at a crossroads together; and the decision I reached sent him in the direction, finally, that his whole life had led up to; he could not escape it. But when I understood what had happened, I took the other road, while I still had the chance. So I'm grateful to Harris Gruener and sorry for him, too. "There is a tide," all right, but whether a man should take it or not depends on where he wants to go.

BEHIND THE NEWS

No one knew how the false and slanderous item on Police Chief Quayle got into the *Clarion*. The editor accepted all blame. It was Friday, press day, in the final lull before the old flat-bed press began clanking out the weekly twelve hundred copies, and everything in the one-room frame building seemed normal. Grinning insanely, young Johnny Deutsch, owner and editor, sat before a typewriter at a roll-top desk near his secretary—all three of which had been his father's before him. He sat as he did each week, his long, loose-jointed body hunched over the old machine, his big hands flying over the keys; then he flung himself back in his chair and read aloud what he had just written. " 'Police Chief Slain by Wolf Pack!' " he cried.

"An immature form of wish fulfillment," his secretary, Miss Gerraghty, murmured acidly—as she did each week.

Ignoring this, Johnny pounded at his typewriter again, the carriage jouncing. Then he threw himself back once more, a lock of jet-black hair dropping onto his forehead, his lean, roughhewn face happy, his brown eyes dancing. " 'This morning,' " he read, " 'Police Chief Wendall E. Quayle was set upon and slain by a mysterious pack of wolves that suddenly appeared on Culver Street. Before the eyes of horrified shoppers, the maddened animals tore Quayle to tattered shreds within seconds.' "

The *Clarion's* printer, Nate Rubin, an ink-smudged youth in blue denim apron, stood at his worktable, setting the back-page supermarket ad and, as he did each week, mournfully shaking his head at the prices. "Johnny"—he glanced up—"Quayle's a slob, but harmless. What you got against him?"

"Nothing personal." Johnny grinned. "But I'm a cop hater," he shouted, "as all true Americans instinctively are. A foe from birth of officialdom, bureaucracy and the heel of tyranny!" Nate considered this, then nodded in agreement and understanding.

Johnny's typewriter clattered again for a time, then stopped. "'Eyewitnesses,'" he read, "'state that the surrounding area was a shambles, while dismembered limbs were found as far south as Yancy Creek. The body was identifiable only from indecent tattoos and the reek of cheap whisky, which characterized our undistinguished late sleuth.'"

This, finally, as also happened each week, was too much for Miss Gerraghty, and peering over her glasses like a benevolent grandmother, she said witheringly, "A mature mind could never, week after week, compose these childlike fantasies to the uproarious amusement of no one but himself. 'Mayor Schimmerhorn Assassinated!'" she quoted contemptuously from a previous effort of Johnny's. "'City Council Wiped Out by Falling Meteor!'" An old memory awakened, she frowned, then shook her head disdainfully. "Meteors." She sniffed. "You're worse than your father."

"What'd he do?" Johnny looked up.

"Lots of things, all foolish. Found an old lump of lead in a field, for one thing, and claimed it was a meteor. Threw it in the lead box on the Linotype machine to melt. Then he ran a story saying it was the first time in history a paper had been printed with type cast from a meteor." In a tone suggesting that both stories were equally absurd, she added, "Same issue that carried your birth announcement," and nodded at the paperweight on Johnny's desk.

Johnny glanced at the paperweight, then picked it up, hefting it absently. It was a rectangle of lead type, the letters worn almost smooth; he hadn't read it for years. But now his eyes scanned the blurred lines that had once announced to four hundred uncaring subscribers that he had been born. When he reached the last sentence, "It is predicted he will make his mark on the world," Johnny's eyes flicked to the date line,

"October 28, 1933." All elation and well-being drained out of him then. He was twenty-three years old, the worn type reminded him, and there wasn't the least indication that he would ever make a mark or even a scratch on the world—and for the first time he was impressed with Miss Gerraghty's weekly tirade.

Recalling his idea, at University Journalism School a few years before, of what life as a newspaperman would be, he smiled bitterly, contrasting that picture with the life he now led. Owner by inheritance of a small-town weekly, its columns filled with stale and newsless news as boring to himself as to his subscribers, he reflected that Miss Gerraghty's contempt was deserved. For he simply went on, week after week, doing nothing to relieve his frustration but compose childish parodies of nonexistent news. He thought of a classmate, now a copy writer for a large advertising agency, earning an enormous salary. Then, with even greater longing, he thought of two other classmates, both of whom were actually married, he reflected bitterly. Glancing at the half-full sheet of copy paper in his typewriter, he felt with sudden force that he was just what Miss Gerraghty said he was, immature and childlike; and he looked down at the worn type in his hand with distaste. The very fact that he had kept it, he suddenly realized, could undoubtedly be explained by Miss Gerraghty in unpleasantly Freudian terms.

On impulse, a new will toward maturity flaming within him, Johnny stood up, walked to the Linotype machine, lifted the cover of the lead box, and dropped his paperweight into the molten metal. "Miss Gerraghty," he said firmly, his voice several tones deeper, "what would a mature mind compose?"

She glanced up, surprised. "If anything," she said, "something at least distantly linked to the remotely possible." Then she turned back to her proof sheets.

Back at his desk after several minutes of frowning thought, his face set, he believed, in new lines of maturity, Johnny typed "Police Chief Loses Pants." Then he went on, typing slowly, to compose a brief fictitious account of an attack on Police Chief Quayle by a large Dalmatian who, Johnny wrote, had torn out the seat of Quayle's pants. But he felt no urge to read this aloud. As he recalled later, Johnny yanked the sheet of paper from his typewriter, tossed it onto his desk, and then left, feeling depressed, for City Hall, informing his staff, who knew better, that he was going to hunt up some last-minute news.

The item appeared on page one, headline and all, just as Johnny had typed it. How it had gotten in with the remaining unset front-page items, no one knew. But it had, and Nate—with his astounding ability to set words and sentences, editing their spelling and punctuation, yet allowing no glimmer of their meaning to touch his mind—had turned it into type along with the others.

In any case, it was Johnny's responsibility to check the issue before the final press run, and he had not done so. Deprived by Miss Gerraghty of even the pretense that the *Clarion* might sometime carry a piece of news worth reading, he had lingered too long talking to the town clerk. This was Miss Miriam Zeebley, a blonde, lithe young woman who resembled Grace Kelly from the shoulders up, though better-looking; Anita Ekberg from waist to shoulders, though less flat-chested; and for the rest of her five feet six inches, as Marilyn Monroe as Miss Monroe undoubtedly wished she looked.

Seated at her desk, in a thin summer dress—polite, cordial enough, but coolly official—Miss Zeebley obviously didn't actually know or care that Johnny Deutsch was alive, and he didn't blame her. There were times when Johnny, staring into his mirror, could convince himself for as long as two or three seconds that he had a sort of offbeat, Lincolnesque good looks. But now, he felt his face flush as the certainty swept over him that he was actually an awkward, crag-faced lout. Then, grateful for even the crumbs of her attention, but knowing that for her anything less than a young Ronald Colman was absurd, he left.

Back at his desk, the *Clarion* already delivered into the official hands of the post office, Johnny reached the lowest ebb of his life. Staring numbly at the page-one libel on Police Chief Quale, knowing that any jury would regard it as tending to "embarrass, humiliate and defame," he knew too that he was a failure and a misfit, inept in life, libel and love; and he considered simply walking to the edge of town, jumping a freight, and beginning life anew in the West.

The front door opened, and a small boy, wearing cowboy boots, the dress jacket of a full colonel in the Space Patrol, and a fluorescent green stocking cap, stepped into the office. He said, "Hey, Johnny, you got some old type I can have for my newspaper?"

"Ask Nate." Johnny gestured wearily at the shabby sink at which Nate was scrubbing his forearms.

"Okay." The boy suddenly grinned. "Gee, it was funny. I sure laughed," he said.

"What was funny?"

"Chief Quayle. Gettin' the seat of his pants tore off. Gee, it was funny; I sure laughed."

"Oh." Johnny nodded. "You've read the story?"

The boy shook his head. "No. I saw it."

"Saw *what?*" Johnny said irritably.

"Saw the dog," the boy explained patiently, "bite off his pants. Gee, it was funny." He laughed. "I sure laughed."

Johnny pushed himself upright in his chair. "You *saw* this happen?"

"Yeah."

"Where?"

"On Culver Street."

"You actually *saw* the dog tear the seat out of Quayle's pants?"

"Yep." The boy grinned. "Gee, it was—"

"When?"

"I dunno." He shrugged. "Few minutes ago. He ran all the way back to the station house. It was sure funny. Everybody laughed like anyth—"

Grabbing the boy by both shoulders, his voice grown low and tense, Johnny said slowly, *"What kind of dog was it?"*

"I dunno," the boy answered without interest. "One of them big white dogs with black spots all over." He turned toward the sink at the back of the room. "Hey, Nate!" he called. "Johnny says for you to gimme some type."

For a full quarter minute Miss Gerraghty just stared at Johnny. Then she blinked her eyes and announced firmly, "Coincidence. An astonishing, yet mathematically predictable coinci—"

Johnny slowly shook his head. "No," he said numbly, his eyes astonished. "It was no coincidence, as any but the scientific mind would know." He turned slowly toward Miss Gerraghty, and in his eyes a glow of triumph was kindling. "Miss Gerraghty," he said slowly, "I don't know how it happened, but what I wrote and printed in the *Clarion* came true. Immediately, and in every detail." Suddenly he grinned, snatching up a fresh sheet of paper, rolled it into his typewriter, and said, "And nothing in the world is going to stop me from trying it again!"

His eyes glittering, staring through the paper at a suddenly glorious and incredible future, Johnny typed "Engagement Announced!" The keys beat out a furious splatter of sound. "Miss Miriam Zeebley to Wed Editor Deutsch!" The type bars jammed, and Johnny frantically pried them apart, then continued. "Town Clerk Zeebley, unexpectedly resigning her position, announced today—"

One week later, the *Clarion* printed, addressed, carried to the post office, and even then, Johnny knew, being delivered, he sat at his desk waiting. Then, as he had hoped, the phone rang; and as he had also hoped, it was Miss Zeebley, her voice lovely as a temple bell. For a full minute Johnny sat listening. Once he said, "But Miss Zeebley, it was an acci—" A few moments later he began, "Typographical err—" During the one time she paused for breath, Johnny managed to say feebly, "It must have been some kind of—joke. A disgruntled employee." Presently, voice dulled and hopeless, he said, "Yes, I'll publish a retraction," and hung up.

For a while, lost in despair, Johnny sat with his head in his hands, staring down at the floor. Then, as some men turn to drink, others to drugs, women, or gambling, Johnny turned to his typewriter. "Quayle Slain by Thug," he typed despondently. "Early this morning," he continued, "the decapitated body of Police Chief Wendall E. Quayle was discovered in an abandoned trunk. Minutes later, his head, shrunken to a fraction of its normal six-and-one-eighth-inch size—"

Presently he tossed the finished story onto Miss Gerraghty's desk. "It came true once," he said sadly, "about Quayle's pants. If I'd only printed this instead."

"It wouldn't have come true then," Miss Gerraghty said, glancing at the headline. "Any more than Miriam Zeebley marrying you. There are some things that are just too ridiculous."

Johnny stared at her for several seconds, his eyes narrowing. "Yeah," he said then, interest and excitement beginning to well up in his voice, "maybe that's it." He nodded thoughtfully. "It's got to be possible, at least; maybe that's the key. You can't go *too* far, you can't go overboard." Suddenly he was elated. "You've hit it, Miss Gerraghty!" He reached for a fresh sheet of copy paper.

As Miss Gerraghty stared at him in icy, unbelieving contempt, Johnny, choosing his words slowly and carefully, began to type. "Among those attending the Old Nakomis Country Club Soirée tonight," he wrote, "will be Miss Miriam Zeebley. It will surprise none who know our ever-popular town clerk to learn that, bearing no malice for an unfortunate error that appeared in these columns recently, she will attend escorted by Ye Ed, Johnny Deutsch."

He pulled the sheet of paper from his machine, dated it in pencil for the following week's issue, scribbled "Social Notes" at the top, then read it through again. "Possible," he murmured approvingly. "Or at least barely within the borders of conceivability." His eyes happy again, Johnny glanced at Miss Gerraghty and grinned. "Shoot the works," he said, and rolled another sheet into his typewriter.

"Psychotic," Miss Gerraghty murmured, nodding soberly. "Like father, like son."

"How do you spell 'bubonic plague'?" Johnny asked, then hastily added, "Never mind; I'd better make it mumps."

The following Saturday Johnny picked up the phone. Miss Gerraghty laid down her proof sheets to listen.

"Miriam," Johnny said presently into the phone, his voice brisk and confident, "I want you to attend the Old Nakomis Country Club Soirée tonight; with me." He leaned back in his chair, feet up on his typewriter, listening. "You have a date? Well, break it," he said firmly. A moment later he smiled and said, "Fine. I'll call for you at eight." There was a pause; then Johnny said, "Quayle, eh? What's the trouble?" Then he nodded. "Thanks; the story'll be in this issue." He replaced the phone, turned to Miss Gerraghty, and waited, humming softly.

For a moment there was no sound in the room; Miss Gerraghty simply stared. Then in a small, frightened voice, she asked, "Is Quayle sick?" Johnny nodded. "Mumps?" Miss Gerraghty whispered.

"Yeah," Johnny said, and turned happily to his typewriter.

The quality and interest of the *Clarion's* news picked up sharply in the weeks that followed. With invariable accuracy, the *Clarion* reported that Miss Miriam Zeebley was attending the Flower and Garden Show, the movies, the Women's Club annual bazaar, a traveling carnival, and the Spelling-Bee State Semi-finals, all with Johnny Deutsch. In addition, the *Clarion* uncannily announced almost simultaneously with the events themselves that Mayor Schimmerhorn was stung by a swarm of bees, and that the City Council, refreshing themselves with cheese sandwiches after a meeting, was stricken to a man with food poisoning. It was predicted by the *Clarion* that the Girl Scouts would sell 42 per cent more cookies than last year in their annual drive, and this came precisely true. The *Clarion* reported that the Old Nakomis Country Club had elected a new vice-president, Johnny Deutsch, and that Police Chief Wendall E. Quayle, having recovered from the mumps, had promptly come down with hives. Circulation increased by leaps and bounds.

For however it happened and whatever the cause, it was undeniably true that what the *Clarion* printed as fact or prediction always came true—so long as Johnny kept his inventions to the reasonably possible.

Once, in his zeal, he violated this principle, and had to rush an extra edition into print on the following day carrying a retraction of the *Clarion's* lead story that Mayor Schimmerhorn, a notorious teetotaler, had been arrested while drunk for peddling indecent post cards in the alley back of City Hall. But, the retraction added, His Honor, understanding how such an error could easily occur, had no intention of suing the *Clarion;* and the mayor explained to friends later that day, his voice faintly puzzled, that this was quite true.

A few days later, Thursday, a hot afternoon in August, Johnny leaned back in his chair, folded his hands complacently in back of his head, lifted his long lean legs up onto his typewriter, and looked across the little office at Miss Gerraghty. She was sitting, chin in hand, listening to a portable radio on her desk from which a voice was saying, ". . . sacred trust to the American people!" A burst of applause followed this statement, and Johnny nodded at the radio and said, "You know, we have seldom carried national news. We've been more of a local paper."

Miss Gerraghty glanced up, nodded absently, then returned her attention to the radio, as the voice resumed solemnly, "In the immortal words of Thomas Jefferson . . ."

"There is no reason," Johnny continued quietly, "why we shouldn't, though. Once in a while." Miss Gerraghty didn't bother to answer. "It might be fun," Johnny added, nodding at the radio. "with the Democratic convention going on, to score a news beat on the rest of the world."

Miss Gerraghty looked at him, faintly puzzled; then her jaw dropped, and she hastily switched off the radio. "No!" She stared at him wide-eyed. Then, voice frightened and ominous, she said, "No, Johnny, you're going too far. Stick to local—"

He was shaking his head. "There are several possible candidates for the Democratic nomination," he said, nodding at the radio, "and it's time to do something about it." Dropping his feet to the floor, Johnny sat up and rolled a fresh sheet of paper into his typewriter. "Think it's all right if we issue the paper a day early?"

"Nobody will notice the difference," Miss Gerraghty replied faintly, as Johnny poised his fingers over the typewriter.

"We'll get the paper to the post office tonight then," he said, "to be delivered in the morning mail. "Kefauver, Stevenson, or Harriman," he murmured, "I just can't make up my mind." Then he suddenly typed, "Stevenson Nominated!" and said, "Think I'll make it on the first ballot."

The next day, the radio blaring with the voice of the excited announcer above the background pandemonium of cheering delegates, Miss Gerraghty looked up at Johnny. "Anybody could have predicted that."

But Johnny wasn't listening. Hands clasped behind his head, staring dreamily at the ceiling, he was murmuring, "It's Ike for President, of course, but whom shall I give the second spot to?"

Seven days later, the radio on Miss Gerraghty's desk blared that Richard Nixon had been given the Republican nomination for vice-president; in precisely the way Johnny's lead story in the *Clarion* had described. Miss Gerraghty wrung her hands, and moaned. "Johnny," she said pitifully, "why?" She snatched a copy of the *Clarion* from her desk, and shook it violently in his face. "Nixon to Run with Ike!" the headline cried. "*Why* does it work?" Miss Gerraghty begged.

"Why, I thought you knew." Johnny looked at her, genuinely surprised. "I thought you'd guessed; don't you ever read science fiction? It's the meteor, Miss Gerraghty."

"The meteor?"

"The one my father found," Johnny said patiently. "It seems to be lead, but actually it was an unknown metal from another world. And somehow, when you turn it into type, the news it prints comes true. Within reason."

"But where did you get—"

"My birth announcement," he said impatiently. "It was cast from the meteor, as you yourself told me. It was saved all these years, till I melted it with the Linotype lead." Johnny shrugged, smiling happily. "And since we remelt our type after each issue, it's always still there, hard at work, issue after issue of the *Clarion*."

Her voice dulled, finally accepting this, Miss Gerraghty said, "But how? Johnny, *how* does it wor—"

"Miss Gerraghty," Johnny said sternly, "if you had ever read science fiction, you'd know that the dullest part is always the explanation. It bores the reader and clutters up the story. Especially when the author flunked high-school physics and simply doesn't know how it works. We'll just skip that," he said firmly, "and get on to more important things. We've got lots to do now."

But in the weeks following the conventions, to Miss Gerraghty's great relief, Johnny's mind turned from the national scene. For while it was delightfully true that Miss Miriam Zeebley and Editor Deutsch continued to do everything mentioned in the *Clarion's* Social Notes, there was a limit to what could be mentioned. Johnny Deutsch was healthy, normal and reasonably full of animal vigor; and while he enjoyed escorting Miriam to the town's social functions, there were times—twenty-four hours a day, in fact—when he longed for more than he could describe in type. He would have liked, for example, to kiss Miss Zeebley, long and lingeringly, full on the lips.

He considered printing this as a news item and burying it among the legal notices at the back of the *Clarion,* but he couldn't quite work up the nerve to do it. He also considered simply kissing Miriam on his own some night; but he couldn't work up the nerve to try this, either. There were times now when, shaving before a date with Miriam, he managed to convince himself for a full minute or more that he was actually a rather rugged, good-looking man. There were even times when he felt that Miriam agreed. But these times never coincided with opportunities to kiss her. At those moments he always knew, with depressing certainty, that he was a gibbering clod. Once again he was a frustrated man, and it seemed to Johnny as the summer went on that his activities with Miriam were forever doomed to those that could be described in a family newspaper.

And so it was, one fine fall morning, that when Miss Gerraghty said, "Did you vote today?" Johnny only looked at her blankly.

"Vote?" he said.

"Today," Miss Gerraghty said patiently, "is Election Day; your first opportunity to help elect a President."

He glanced at the wall calendar. Miss Gerraghty was right. "Thanks," he said, and his face cleared. "Thanks for reminding me"—once again his voice was brisk and assured—"or I might have been too late."

"Too late for what?"

"To make sure," Johnny said, reaching for a sheet of copy paper, "that the right man is elected."

Slowly Miss Gerraghty rose from her desk, walked around it, and stood facing Johnny. "No," she said quietly.

"What do you mean?" He looked up.

"I won't let you, Johnny. That's one thing neither you nor anyone else is going to interfere with."

He sat back in his chair, smiling up at her. "Don't you want to see the right man elected?"

"Certainly," she said, "but who is he? That's something no less than seventy million Americans are competent to decide." Her voice rose shrilly. "You hear me, Johnny? You let this alone!"

For a moment he sat staring up at her, and Miss Gerraghty realized how much he still resembled the boy he had been only a few years ago. "Don't be silly, Miss Gerraghty," he said, and turned to his typewriter. "Not many people would pass up this chance."

"And that," Miss Gerraghty said—and now she was speaking more to herself than to Johnny—"may be what is wrong with the world today." She walked back to her desk and for the rest of the morning sat thinking. She considered, first, burning down the office, but she knew she would be stopped. Then she considered rushing out to buttonhole people on the street and tell them the secret only the staff shared about the *Clarion;* but she knew she would not be believed. For a wild moment she considered murder, but knew immediately that she could never harm a hair of Johnny Deutsch's head.

At noon, when Johnny and Nate left for lunch, Miss Gerraghty stayed behind. The moment the door closed she stood up and walked to the files. For the next hour and a half, her fingers working frantically, her face soon perspiring and dust-streaked, she hunted desperately through the files.

"What are you doing?" Johnny asked, as he opened the office door on his return from lunch. Miss Gerraghty turned, her old body moving with a terrible weariness, her face like granite. From the top of the old wood filing cabinets, she picked up a stack of newspapers, and nodded at them somberly.

"I have been going through the back files," she answered. For a moment, her eyes like embers, she stared across the room at Johnny. "Has it occurred to you," she burst out bitterly, "that you weren't the first to use that meteor for type?" She dropped the stack of papers on Johnny's desk; their edges, he saw, were yellowed and crumbling with age. "Your father used it first, remember!" Her bony forefinger, trembling violently, touched a faded column of type. "Read it! Like you, he wasn't afraid to deal with subjects he knew nothing about!"

Johnny leaned forward to study the old story; after a moment he glanced at her, puzzled. "It's nothing," he said. "Just a column of speculation on financial affairs. Harmless stuff."

"Harmless! 'Stocks will go down,' the old idiot wrote, just as though he knew what he was talking about! And of course it came true. Oh, it came true, all right! Look at that date!" Her shaking finger touched the date line. " 'October 28, 1929,' and the next day the stock market crashed and the worst depression in mankind's history began."

She snatched the old paper from the stack, revealing the next. "Presently," she said with acid quietness, "our genius turned to politics, just as his son wants to do. But he jumped into *world* politics, with an asinine editorial on Pacific developments." Her bony forefinger pointed out the date line. " 'September 17, 1931,' and of course his story came true, in a way he never realized. Japan invaded Manchuria the very next day! Two years later"—she revealed the next paper—"he wrote an empty-headed article on German politics, and Hitler became Chancellor of the Third Reich! In the very same year"—she pointed to another yellowing page—"he very nearly got Roosevelt assassinated, and"—her finger stabbed at still another story signed by Johnny's father—"read this and you'll see that he was directly responsible for the Dionne quintuplets!"

For a full fifteen seconds there was no sound in the little office but the chattering of Johnny's teeth. Then, barely able to speak, he whispered pitifully, "What about—World War Two?"

In a tone almost of kindness, Miss Gerraghty said, "No. I've checked the files carefully, and he wasn't responsible. But he did plenty! Any number of floods, fires, earthquakes and minor holocausts I haven't even bothered to mention! And he never realized it, never saw the connection, and I didn't either, till now. In time, I guess, the meteor metal thinned out. New lead was added to the Linotype from time to time, of course, and by the late 'thirties, as far as I can tell from the files, there wasn't enough meteor metal left to do any harm. Until you melted some of that original type again—your birth announcement, cast in full-strength meteor metal! Johnny"—her voice deepened with implacable authority—"you've got to clean out the lead box on the Linotype machine and throw out every scrap of old lead in the place. Right *now!*"

His voice a humble whisper, Johnny said, "Yes. Of course. Right away. Just as soon as I run one last story—"

"No!"

"—about my elopement!" he said frantically. "I finally figured out what to do about Miriam and the story is all ready to set up!"

For a full minute Miss Gerraghty considered. Then finally, reluctantly, she said, "All right; though I'm very fond of Miriam. And I think it's criminal to risk another generation of Deutschs. This one last story—and that's all!"

"Okay," Johnny said humbly. Then, physically and emotionally exhausted, Miss Gerraghty went home for the day, while Johnny allowed the presidential election of 1956 to proceed normally.

But he did write still one more story, which he personally set up in meteor type. Then he dropped every other scrap of type metal in the office into the deepest part of Yancy Creek. This final story, a little square of type locked in the office safe, has not yet been printed. It announces the birth of Johnny's daughter, giving precise details of her weight and length and stating that she resembles her mother exactly. Since obviously the prediction had come true in his own case, Johnny added, "It is predicted that she will make her mark on the world." Then he dated the story exactly nine months later than the elopement announcement.

Whether this final story will come true or not— whether the meteor metal from an unknown world will continue to have its mysterious effect—it is impossible to say. But it still *seems* to be working okay so far; at least, Miriam Deutsch is expecting.

QUIT ZOOMIN' THOSE HANDS
THROUGH THE AIR

Hey, quit zoomin' your *hands* through the air, boy— I know you was a flier! You flew *good* in the war, course you did; I'd expect that from a grandson of mine. But don't get to thinking you know all about war, son, or flying machines either. The war we finished in 'sixty-five is still the toughest we've fought, and don't you forget it. It was a big war fought by

big men, and your Pattons and Arnolds and Stilwells
—they were *good,* boy, no denying it—but Grant, there
was a general. Never told you about this before, because I was swore to secrecy by the general himself,
but I think it's all right, now; I think the oath has
expired. Now, *quiet,* boy! Put those hands in your
pockets and listen!

Now, the night I'm talking about, the night I met
the general, I didn't know we'd see him at all. Didn't
know anything except we were riding along Pennsylvania Avenue, me and the major, him not saying
where we were going or why, just jogging along, one
hand on the reins, a big black box strapped to the
major's saddle in front, and that little pointy beard of
his stabbing up and down with every step.

It was late, after ten, and everyone was asleep. But
the moon was up, bright and full through the trees,
and it was nice—the horses' shadows gliding along
sharp and clear beside us, and not a sound in the street
but their hoofs, hollow on the packed dirt. We'd been
riding two days, I'd been nipping some liberated applejack—only we didn't say "liberated" then; we called it
"foraging"—and I was asleep in the saddle, my trumpet
jiggling in the small of my back. Then the major
nudged me, and I woke up and saw the White House
ahead. "Yessir," I said.

He looked at me, the moon shining yellow on his
epaulets, and said, real quiet, "Tonight, boy, we may
win the war. You and I." He smiled, mysterious, and
patted the black box. "You know who I am, boy?"

"Yessir."

"No, you don't. I'm a professor. Up at Harvard
College. Or was, anyway. Glad to be in the army now,
though. Pack of fools up there, most of them; can't
see past the ends of their noses. Well, tonight, boy,
we may win the war."

"Yessir," I said. Most officers higher than captain were a little queer in the head, I'd noticed, majors especially. That's how it was then, anyway, and I don't reckon it's changed any, even in the Air Force.

We stopped near the White House at the edge of the lawn and sat looking at it—a great big old house, silvery white in the moonlight, the light over the front door shining out through the porch columns onto the driveway. There was a light in an east window on the ground floor, and I kept hoping I'd see the President, but I didn't. The major opened his box. "Know what this is, boy?"

"Nosir."

"It's my own invention, based on my own theories, nobody else's. They think I'm a crackpot up at the School, but I think it'll work. Win the war, boy." He moved a little lever inside the box. "Don't want to send us too far ahead, son, or technical progress will be beyond us. Say ninety years or so from now, approximately; think that ought to be about right?"

"Yessir."

"All right." The major jammed his thumb down on a little button in the box; it made a humming sound that kept rising higher and higher till my ears began to hurt; then he lifted his hand. "Well," he said, smiling and nodding, the little pointy beard going up and down, "it is now some ninety-odd years later." He nodded at the White House. "Glad to see it's still standing."

I looked up at the White House again. It was just the same, the light still shining out between the big white columns, but I didn't say anything.

The major twitched his reins and turned. "Well, boy, we've got work ahead; come on." And he set off at a trot along Pennsylvania Avenue with me beside him. Pretty soon we turned south, and the major twisted around in his saddle and said, "Now, the question is, what do they have in the future?" He held up his finger like a teacher in school, and I believed the part about him being a professor. "We don't know," the major went on, "but we know where to find it. In a museum. We're going to the Smithsonian Institution, if it's still standing. For us it should be a veritable storehouse of the future."

It had been standing last week, I knew, and after a while, off across the grass to the east, there it was, a stone building with towers like a castle, looking just the same as always, the windows now blank and white in the moonlight. "Still standing, sir," I said.

"Good," said the major. "Reconnaissance approach, now," and we went on to a cross street and turned into it. Up ahead were several buildings I'd never noticed before, and we went up to them and swung down off our horses. "Walk between these buildings," the major said, leading his horse. "Quiet, now; we're reconnoitering."

We crept on, quiet as could be, in the shadows between the two buildings. The one to the right looked just like the Smithsonian to me, and I knew it must be a part of it; another building I'd never seen before. The major was all excited now, and kept whispering. "Some new kind of weapon that will destroy the whole Rebel Army is what we're looking for. Let me know if you see any such thing, boy."

"Yessir," I said, and I almost bumped into something out there in the open in front of the building at the left. It was big and made entirely out of heavy metal, and instead of wheels it rested on two movable belts made of metal; big flat plates linked together.

"Looks like a tank," said the major, "though I don't know what they keep in it. Keep moving, boy; this thing is obviously no use on a battlefield."

We walked on just a step, and there on the pavement in front of us was a tremendous cannon, three times bigger than any I'd ever seen before in my life. It had an immense long barrel, wheels high as my chest, and it was painted kind of funny, in wavy stripes and splotches, so that you could hardly see it at first in the moonlight that got down between the buildings. *"Look* at that thing!" the major said softly. "It would pulverize Lee in an hour, but I don't know how we'd carry it. No," he said, shaking his head, "this isn't it. I wonder what they've got inside, though." He stepped up to the doors and peered in through the glass, shading his eyes with his hand. Then he gasped and turned to me.

I went up beside him and looked through the glass. It was a long, big building, the moonlight slanting in through the windows all along one side; and all over the floor, and even hanging from the ceiling, were the weirdest-looking things I ever saw. They were each big as a wagon, some bigger, and they had wheels, but only two wheels, near the front; and I was trying to figure that out when the major got his voice back.

"Aircraft, by God!" he said. "They've got aircraft! Win the war!"

"Air what, sir?"

"Aircraft. Flying machines. They fly through the air. Don't you see the wings, boy?"

Each of the machines I could see inside had two things sticking out at each side like oversize ironing boards, but they looked stiff to me, and I didn't see how they could flap like wings. I didn't know what else the major could be talking about, though. "Yessir," I said.

But the major was shaking his head again. "Much too advanced," he said. "We could never master them.

What we need is an earlier type, and I don't see any in here. Come on, boy; don't straggle."

We walked on, leading the horses, toward the front of the other building. At the doors we peeked in, and there on the floor, with tools and empty crates lying around as though they'd just unpacked it, was another of the things, a flying machine. Only this was far smaller, and was nothing but a framework of wood like a big box kite, with little canvas wings, as the major called them. It didn't have wheels, either, just a couple of runners like a sled. Lying propped against a wall, as though they were just ready to put it up, was a sign. The moonlight didn't quite reach it, and I couldn't read all the words, but I could make out a few. "World's first," it said in one place, and farther down it said, "Kitty Hawk."

The major just stood there for maybe a minute, staring like a man in a trance. Then he murmured to himself. "Very like sketches of da Vinci's model; only apparently this one worked." He grinned suddenly, all excited. "This is it, boy," he said. "This is why we came."

I knew what he had in mind, and I didn't like it. "You'll never break in there, sir," I said. "Those doors look mighty solid, and I'll bet this place is guarded like the mint."

The major just smiled, mysterious again. "Of course it is, son; it's the treasure house of a nation. No one could possibly get in with any hope of removing anything, let alone this aircraft—under ordinary circumstances. But don't worry about that, boy; just leave it to me. Right now we need fuel." Turning on his heel, he walked back to his horse, took the reins, and led him off; and I followed with mine.

Off some distance, under some trees, near a big open space like a park, the major set the lever inside his black box, and pressed the button. "Back in eighteen sixty-four, now," he said then, and sniffed. "Air smells fresher. Now, I want you to take your horse, go to garrison headquarters, and bring back all the petrol you can carry. They've got some for cleaning uniforms. Tell them I'll take full responsibility. Understand?"

"Yessir."

"Then off with you. When you come back, this is where I want you to meet me." The major turned and began walking away with his horse.

At headquarters the guard woke a private, who woke a corporal, who woke a sergeant, who woke a lieutenant, who woke a captain, who swore a little and then woke up the private again and told him to give me what I wanted. The private went away, murmuring softly to himself, and came back pretty soon with six five-gallon jugs; and I tied them to my saddle, signed six sets of receipts in triplicate, and led my horse back through the moonlit streets of Washington, taking a nip of applejack now and then.

I went by the White House again, on purpose; and this time someone was standing silhouetted against the lighted east window—a big man, tall and thin, his shoulders bowed, his head down on his chest—and I couldn't help but get the impression of a weary strength and purpose and a tremendous dignity. I felt sure it was him, but I can't rightly claim I saw the President, because I've always been one to stick to the facts and never stretch the truth even a little bit.

The major was waiting under the trees, and my jaw nearly dropped off, because the flying machine was sitting beside him. "Sir," I said "how did you—"

The major interrupted, smiling and stroking his little beard: "Very simple. I merely stood at the front door"'—he patted the black box at the saddle near his shoulder—"and moved back in time to a moment when even the Smithsonian didn't exist. Then I stepped a few paces ahead with the box under my arm, adjusted the lever again, moved forward to the proper moment, and there I was, standing beside the flying machine. I took myself and the machine out by the same method, and my mount pulled it here on its skids."

"Yessir," I said. I figured I could keep up this foolishness as long as he could, though I did wonder how he had got the flying machine out.

The major pointed ahead. "I've been exploring the ground, and it's pretty rocky and rough." He turned to the black box, adjusted the dial, and pressed the button. "Now, it's a park," he said, "sometime in the nineteen forties."

"Yessir," I said.

The major nodded at a little spout in the flying machine. "Fill her up," he said, and I untied one of the jugs, uncorked it, and began to pour. The tank sounded dry when the petrol hit it, and a cloud of dust puffed up from the spout. It didn't hold very much, only a few quarts, and the major began untying the other jugs. "Lash these down in the machine," he said, and while I was doing that, the major began pacing up and down, muttering to himself. "To start the engine, I should imagine you simply turn the propellers. But the machine will need help in getting into the air." He kept walking up and down, pulling his beard; then he nodded his head. "Yes," he said, "that should do it, I think." He stopped and looked at me. "Nerves in good shape, boy? Hands steady and reliable?"

"Yessir."

"All right, son, this thing should be easy to fly— mostly a matter of balance, I imagine." He pointed to a sort of saddle at the front of the machine. "I believe you simply lie on your stomach with your hips in this saddle; it connects with the rudder and wings by cables. By merely moving from side to side, you control the machine's balance and direction." The major pointed to a lever. "Work this with your hand," he said, "to go up or down. That's all there is to it, so far as I can see, and if I'm wrong in any details, you can correct them in the air with a little experimenting. Think you can fly it, boy?"

"Yessir."

"Good," he said, and grabbed one of the propellers at the back and began turning it. I worked on the other propeller, but nothing happened; they just creaked, stiff and rusty-like. But we kept turning, yanking harder and harder, and pretty soon the little engine coughed.

"Now, *heave*, boy!" the major said, and we laid into it hard, and every time, now, the engine would cough a little. Finally, we yanked so hard, both together, our feet nearly came off the ground, and the motor coughed and kept on coughing and like to choked to death. Then it sort of cleared its throat and started to stutter but didn't stop, and then it was running smooth, the propellers just whirling, flashing and shining in the moonlight till you could hardly see them, and the flying machine shaking like a wet dog, with little clouds of dust pouring up out of every part of it.

"Excellent," said the major, and he sneezed from the dust. Then he began unfastening the horses' bridles, strapping them together again to make a single long rein. He posed the horses in front of the machine and said, "Get in, boy. We've got a busy night ahead." I lay down in the saddle, and he climbed up on the top wing and lay down on his stomach. "You take the lever, and I'll take the rein. Ready, boy?"

"Yessir."

"*Gee up!*" said the major, snapping the rein hard, and the horses started off, heads down, hoofs digging in.

The flying machine sort of bumped along over the grass on its skids, but it soon smoothed out and began sliding along, level as a sled on packed snow, and the horses' heads came up and they began to trot, the motor just chugging away.

"Sound *forward!*" said the major, and I unslung my trumpet and blew forward; the horses buckled into it, and we were skimming along, must have been fifteen, maybe twenty miles an hour or even faster.

"Now, *charge!*" yelled the major, and I blew charge, and the hoofs began drumming the turf, the horses whinnying and snorting, the engine chugging faster and faster, the propellers whining in back of us, and all of a sudden the grass was a good five feet below, and the reins were hanging straight down. Then—for a second it scared me—we were passing the horses. We were right over their backs; then they began slipping away under the machine, and the major dropped the reins and yelled, "Pull back the lever!" I yanked back hard, and we shot up into the air like a rocket.

I remembered what the major had said about experimenting and tried easing back on the lever, and the flying machine sort of leveled out, and there we were, chugging along faster than I'd ever gone in my life. It was wonderful fun, and I glanced down and there was Washington spread out below, a lot bigger than I'd thought it was and with more lights than I'd known there were in the world. They were *bright,* too; didn't look like candles and kerosene lamps at all. Way off, toward the center of town, some of the lights were red and green, and so bright they lighted up the sky.

"Watch out!" yelled the major, and just ahead,

rushing straight at us, was a tremendous monument or something, a big tall stone needle.

I don't know why, but I twisted hard to the left in the little saddle and yanked back on the lever, and the wing heaved up and the flying machine shot off to one side, the wing tip nearly grazing the monument. Then I lay straight again, holding the lever steady. The machine leveled off, and it was like the first time I drove a team. I could feel in my bones that I was a natural-born flying-machine driver.

"Back to headquarters," said the major. "Can you find the way?"

"Yessir," I said, and headed south.

The major fiddled with the dial in his black box and pressed the button, and down below now, in the moonlight, I could see the dirt road leading out of Washington back to headquarters. I turned for a last look at the city, but there were only a few lights now, not looking nearly as bright as before; the red and green lights were gone.

But the road was bright in the moonlight, and we tore along over it when it went straight, cut across bends when it curved, flying it must have been close to forty miles an hour. The wind streamed back cold, and I pulled out the white knit muffler my grandma gave me and looped it around my throat. One end streamed back, flapping and waving in the wind. I thought my forage cap might blow off, so I reversed it on my head, the peak at the back, and I felt that now I looked the way a flying-machine driver ought to, and wished the girls back home could have seen me.

For a while I practiced with the lever and hip saddle, soaring up till the engine started coughing, and turning and dipping down, seeing how close I could shave the road. But finally the major yelled and made me quit. Every now and then we'd see a light flare up in a farmhouse, and when we'd look back we'd see the light wobbling across the yard and know some farmer was out there with his lamp, staring up at the noise in the sky.

Several times, on the way, we had to fill the tank again, and pretty soon, maybe less than two hours, campfires began sliding under our wings, and the major was leaning from side to side, looking down at the ground. Then he pointed ahead. "That field down there, boy; can you land this thing with the engine off?"

"Yessir," I said, and I stopped the engine, and the machine began sliding down like a toboggan, and I kept easing the lever back and forth, watching the field come up to meet us, growing bigger and bigger every second. We didn't make a sound now, except for the wind sighing through the wires, and we came in like a ghost, the moonlight white on our wings. Our downward path and the edge of the field met exactly, and the instant before we hit, my arm eased the lever back, and the skids touched the grass like a whisper. Then we bumped a little, stopped, and sat there a moment not saying a word. Off in the weeds the crickets began chirping again.

The major said there was a cliff at the side of the field and we found it, and slid the machine over to the edge of it, and then we started walking around the field in opposite directions, looking for a path or sentry. I found the sentry right away, guarding the path lying down with his eyes closed. My applejack was gone, so I shook him awake and explained my problem.

"How much you got?" he said; I told him a dollar, and he went off into the woods and came back with a jug. "Good whisky," he said, "the best. And exactly a dollar's worth; the jug's nearly full." So I tasted the whisky—it *was* good—paid him, took the jug back and tied it down in the machine. Then I went back to the path and called the major, and he came over, cutting across the field. Then the sentry led us down the path toward the general's tent.

It was a square tent with a gabled roof, a lantern burning inside, and the front flap open. The sentry saluted. "Major of Cavalry here, sir." He pronounced the word like an ignorant infantryman. "Says it's secret and urgent."

"Send the *calvary* in," said a voice, pronouncing it just that way, and I knew the general was a horse soldier at heart.

We stepped forward, saluting. The general was sitting on a kitchen chair, his feet, in old army shoes with the laces untied, propped on a big wooden keg with a spigot. He wore a black slouch hat, his vest and uniform blouse were unbuttoned, and I saw three silver stars embroidered on a shoulder strap. The general's eyes were blue, hard and tough, and he wore a full beard. "At ease," he said. "Well?"

"Sir," said the major, "we have a flying machine and propose, with your permission, to use it against the rebs."

"Well," said the general, leaning back on the hind legs of his chair, "you've come in the nick of time. Lee's men are massed at Cold Harbor, and I've been sitting here all night dri—thinking. They've got to be crushed before . . . A *flying* machine, did you say?"

"Yessir," said the major.

"H'mm," said the general. "Where'd you get it?"

"Well, sir, that's a long story."

"I'll bet it is," said the general. He picked up a stub of cigar from the table beside him and chewed it thoughtfully. "If I hadn't been thinking hard and steadily all night, I wouldn't believe a word of this.

What do you propose to do with your flying machine?"

"Load it with grenades!" The major's eyes began to sparkle. "Drop them spang on rebel headquarters! Force immediate surrend—"

The general shook his head. "No," he said, "I don't think so. Air power isn't enough, son, and will never replace the foot soldier, mark my words. Has its place, though, and you've done good work." He glanced at me. "You the driver, son?"

"Yessir."

He turned to the major again. "I want you to go up with a map. Locate Lee's positions. Mark them on the map and return. Do that, major, and tomorrow, June third, after the Battle of Cold Harbor, I'll personally pin silver leaves on your straps. Because I'm going to take Richmond like—well, I don't know what. As for you, son"—he glanced at my stripe—"you'll make corporal. Might even design new badges for you; pair of wings on the chest or something like that."

"Yessir," I said.

"Where's the machine?" said the general. "Believe I'll walk down and look at it. Lead the way." The major and me saluted, turned and walked out, and the general said, "Go ahead; I'll catch up."

At the field the general caught up, shoving something into his hip pocket—a handkerchief, maybe. "Here's your map," he said, and he handed a folded paper to the major.

The major took it, saluted and said, "For the Union, sir! For the cause of—"

"Save the speeches," said the general, "till you're running for office."

"Yessir," said the major, and he turned to me. "Fill her up!"

I filled the tank, we spun the propellers, and this time the engine started right up. We climbed in, and

I reversed my forage cap and tied on my scarf.

"Good," said the general approvingly. "Style; real calvary style."

We shoved off and dropped over the cliff like a dead weight, the ground rushing up fast. Then the wings bit into the air, I pulled back my lever, and we shot up, the engine snorting, fighting for altitude, and I swung out wide and circled the field, once at fifty feet, then at a hundred. The first time, the general just stood there, head back, mouth open, staring up at us, and I could see his brass buttons gleam in the moonlight. The second time around he still had his head back, but I don't think he was looking at us. He had a hand to his mouth, and he was drinking a glass of water—I could tell because just as we straightened and headed south, he threw it off into the bushes hard as he could, and I could see the glass flash in the moonlight. Then he started back to headquarters at a dead run, in a hurry, I guess, to get back to his thinking.

The machine was snorting at the front end, kicking up at the hindquarters, high-spirited, and I had all I could do to keep her from shying, and I wished she'd had reins. Down below, cold and sparkly in the moonlight, I could see the James River, stretching east and west, and the lights of Richmond, but it was no time for sight-seeing. The machine was frisky, trembling in the flanks, and before I knew it she took the bit in her mouth and headed straight down, the wind screaming through her wires, the ripples on the water rushing up at us.

But I'd handled runaways before, and I heaved back on the lever, forcing her head up, and she curved back into the air fast as a calvary mount at a barrier. But this time she didn't cough at the top of the curve. She snorted through her nostrils, wild with power, and I barely had time to yell, "Hang on!" to the major before she went clear over on her back and shot down toward the river again. The major yelled, but the applejack was bubbling inside me and I'd never had such a thrill, and I yelled, too, laughing and screaming. Then I pulled back hard, yelling, "Whoa!" but up and over we went again, the wings creaking like saddle leather on a galloping horse. At the top of the climb, I leaned hard to the left, and we shot off in a wide, beautiful curve, and I never had such fun in my life.

Then she quieted down a little. She wasn't broken, I knew, but she could feel a real rider in the saddle, so she waited, figuring out what to try next. The major got his breath and used it for cursing. He didn't call me anything I'd ever heard before, and I'd been in the calvary since I joined the Army. It was a beautiful job and I admired it. "Yessir," I said when his breath ran out again.

He still had plenty to say, I think, but campfires were sliding under our wings, and he had to get out his map and go to work. We flew back and forth, parallel with the river, the major busy with his pencil and map. It was dull and monotonous for both me and the machine, and I kept wondering if the rebs could see or hear us. So I kept sneaking closer and closer to the ground, and pretty soon, directly ahead in a clearing, I saw a campfire with men around it. I don't rightly know if it was me or the machine had the idea, but I barely touched the lever and she dipped her nose and shot right down, aiming smack at the fire.

They saw us then, all right, and heard us, too. They scattered, yelling and cursing, with me leaning over screaming at them and laughing like mad. I hauled back on the lever maybe five feet from the ground, and the fire singed our tail as we curved back up. But this time, at the top of the climb, the engine got the hiccups, and I had to turn and come down in a slow glide to ease the strain off the engine till she got her breath, and now the men below had muskets out, and they were mad. They fired kneeling, following up with their sights the way you lead ducks, the musket balls whistling past us.

"Come on!" I yelled. I slapped the flying machine on her side, unslung my trumpet, and blew charge. Down we went, the engine neighing and whinnying like crazy, and the men tossed their muskets aside and dived in all directions, and we fanned the flames with our wings and went up like a bullet, the engine screaming in triumph. At the top of the curve I turned, and we shot off over the treetops, the wing tip pointing straight at the moon. "Sorry, sir," I said, before the major could get his breath. "She's wild—feeling her oats. But I think I've got her under control."

"Then get back to headquarters before you kill us," he said coldly. "We'll discuss this later."

"Yessir," I said. I spotted the river off to one side and flew over it, and when the major got us oriented he navigated us back to the field.

"Wait here," he said when we landed, and he trotted down the path toward the general's tent. I was just as glad; I felt like a drink, and besides I loved that machine now and wanted to take care of her. I wiped her down with my muffler, and wished I could feed her something.

Then I felt around inside the machine, and then I was cussing that sentry, beating the major's record, I think, because my whisky was gone, and I knew what that sentry had done: sneaked back to my machine and got it soon as he had me and the major in the general's tent, and now he was back at the guardhouse, probably, lapping it up and laughing at me.

The major came down the path fast. "Back to Washington, and hurry," he said. "Got to get this where it belongs before daylight or the space-time continuum will be broken and no telling what might happen then." So we filled the tank and flew on back to Washington. I was tired and so was the flying machine, I guess, because now she just chugged along, heading for home and the stable.

We landed near the trees again, and climbed out, stiff and tired. And after creaking and sighing a little, the flying machine just sat there on the ground, dead tired, too. There were a couple of musket-ball holes in her wings and some soot on her tail, but otherwise she looked just the same.

"Look alive, boy!" the major said. "You go hunt for the horses, and I'll get the machine back," and he got behind the flying machine and began pushing it along over the grass.

I found the horses grazing not far off, brought them back, and tethered them to the trees. When the major returned we started back, just as dawn was breaking.

Well, I never did get my promotion. Or my wings either. . . . It got hot, and pretty soon I fell asleep.

After a while I heard the major call, "Boy! Boy!" and I woke up saying, "Yessir!" but he didn't mean me. A paper boy was running over with a newspaper, and when the major paid for it, I drew alongside and we both looked at it, sitting there in our saddles near the outskirts of Washington. BATTLE AT COLD HARBOR, it said, and underneath were a lot of smaller headlines one after the other. *Disaster for Union Forces! Surprise Attack at Daybreak Fails! Repulsed in Eight Minutes! Knowledge of Rebel Positions Faulty! Confederate Losses Small, Ours Large, Grant Offers No Explanation; Inquiry Urged!* There was a news story, too, but we didn't read it. The major flung the paper to the gutter and touched his spurs to his horse, and I followed.

By noon the next day we were back in our lines, but we didn't look for the general. We didn't feel any need to, because we felt sure he was looking for us. He never found us, though; possibly because I grew a beard, and the major shaved his off. And we never had told him our names. Well, Grant finally took Richmond—he was a great general—but he had to take it by siege.

I only saw him one more time, and that was years later when he wasn't a general any more. It was a New Year's Day, and I was in Washington and saw a long line of people waiting to get into the White House, and knew it must be the public reception the Presidents used to hold every New Year's. So I stood in line, and an hour later I reached the President. "Remember me, General?" I said.

He stared at me, narrowing his eyes; then his face got red and his eyes flashed. But he took a deep breath, remembering I was a voter, forced a smile, and nodded at a door behind him. "Wait in there," he said.

Soon afterward the reception ended, and the general sat facing me, behind his big desk, biting the end off a short cigar. "Well," he said, without any preliminaries, "what went wrong?"

So I told him; I'd figured it out long since, of course. I told him how the flying machine went crazy, looping till we could hardly see straight, so that we flew north again and mapped our own lines.

"I found that out," said the general, "immediately after ordering the attack." Then I told him about the sentry who'd sold me the whisky, and how I thought he'd stolen it back again, when he hadn't.

The general nodded. "Poured that whisky into the machine, didn't you? Mistook it for a jug of gasoline."

"Yes," I said.

He nodded again. "Naturally the flying machine

went crazy. That was my own private brand of whisky, the same whisky Lincoln spoke of so highly. That damned sentry of mine was stealing it all through the war." He leaned back in his chair, puffing his cigar. "Well," he said, "I guess it's just as well you didn't succeed; Lee thought so, too. We discussed it at Appomattox before the formal surrender, just the two of us chatting in the farmhouse. Never have told anyone what we talked about there, and everybody's been wondering and guessing ever since. Well, we talked about air power, son, and Lee was opposed to it, and so was I. Wars are meant for the ground, boy, and if they ever take to the air they'll start dropping bomb-shells, mark my words, and if they ever do that, there'll be hell to pay. So Lee and I decided to keep our mouths shut about air power, and we have—you won't find a word about it in my memoirs or his. Anyway, son, as Billy Sherman said, 'War is hell,' and there's no sense starting people thinking up ways to make it worse. So I want you to keep quiet about Cold Harbor. Don't say a word if you live to be a hundred."

"Yessir," I said, and I never have. But I'm way past a hundred now, son, and if the general wanted me to keep quiet after that he'd have said so. Now, take those hands out of the air, boy! Wait'll the world's *first* pilot gets through talking!

A DASH OF SPRING

A magazine illustration would never fit this story. For one thing, the girl (her name is Louise Huppfelt) isn't good-looking enough. As for the guy (Ralph Shultz is the name), he's too short, and he wears glasses.

No, Louise Huppfelt and Ralph Shultz are *real-life* people, and—no use denying it—life in the stories is just a little bit different. A lot different, in fact—a lot *better*, and if real life would only get wise to itself, it would imitate slavishly some of the wonderful people who live in the stories. Oh, they have problems, yes, wouldn't you like to trade your problems for theirs? Take the high cost of housing, for example. They have no worries about that. Most of those wonderful people live in big rambling homes, country estates, or beautifully decorated apartments. They're *happy*, and it must be contagious because even the people in the *ads* are happy. All it takes is a can of floor wax. Or give them a new kind of razor blade and they grin with ecstasy. And go crazy with delight over a box of corn flakes. While you, dear reader, a victim of real life, what do *you* do on a rainy Monday morning? You just sit there, like Ralph Shultz or Louise Huppfelt, chewing away on those very same corn flakes with a miserable look on your face.

There's no doubt about it, as Ralph and Louise would be the first to agree, it's time we changed, changed real life to life as it *should* be, life as it's lived in the stories. Maybe that's the solution to world peace. Maybe it isn't, of course, but at least it's as good as a lot of others you read.

Anyway, take a recent issue of a certain very fine magazine. Ralph and Louise both read it, and you probably did, too. On page thirty you saw UNDER THE SKIN. *Can a beautiful, wealthy girl find happiness?*

On the next page was an article: HAS HOLLYWOOD GONE HOLLYWOOD? *A debate by a panel of famous stars.*

And on page thirty-four—here's the one you read first—RECIPE FOR LOVE. *A dash of spring, a boy and a girl . . . and just a pinch of loneliness.*

Now, millions of people read that story, including Ralph Shultz who lives in a boarding house on East Twenty-sixth Street. After supper one night, in his shirt sleeves and wearing a pair of battered old slippers, Ralph sat down in his ancient easy chair, picked up his magazine, leafed through it, looking at the illustrations first, then turned back to RECIPE FOR LOVE and began to read.

There were other empty seats on the bus, he read, *quite a number, in fact. But the other half of this vacant seat was occupied by a girl. Not just a girl, but a girl whose deep red hair picked up and held some of the choicer tints of the late-afternoon sun.*

"Yippee," said Ralph mournfully.

A girl whose eyes, whose soft, brown eyes, were queen-size and touched with flecks of gold.

Ralph whistled through his teeth.

A girl, the tall young man decided, who was very much worth sitting next to. And so, because he was young and because it was spring the young man sat down . . . next to the girl with the beautiful queen-size eyes.

"Yeah," said Ralph, "*I* ride the bus every night and just *show* me a girl like that. And if I did see her, so what? My hair isn't wavy, I barely hit five ten and a half, and I wear glasses besides. *Rimless* glasses. Wonder if horn-rimmed glasses would look more distinguished, maybe?"

Now, hundreds, maybe thousands of other people were reading that story at just about the same time Ralph was. People Ralph had never heard of—Louise Huppfelt, for instance. She was alone, as she often was, in her little two-room apartment on Fortieth Street, not kissing anybody, not wearing a beautiful sea-green gown. She was wearing a rather ratty old bathrobe, in fact, and she'd just washed out her stockings and settled down for a spot of reading.

RECIPE FOR LOVE, she saw, and she sighed and said, "Brother, that's just what I need."

There were other empty seats on the bus, quite a number, in fact. But the other half of this vacant seat—

"Don't tell me," said Louise.

—was occupied by a girl.

"Surprise, surprise."

A girl whose deep-red hair—

"Don't they *ever* have plain, brown hair like mine?"

—whose deep-red hair picked up and held some of the choicer tints of the late-afternoon sun.

"All my hair ever picks up are some of the choicer tints of New York soot."

Her soft, brown eyes, were queen-size and touched with flecks of gold.

"Oh, brother!" said Louise. "And what does *he* look like—our hero? Tell me quick! I just can't *wait!*"

Down on Twenty-sixth Street, Ralph Shultz, his feet up on the bed now, slouched down in the easy chair and read *Continued on page 78.*

Ralph turned the pages and read: *The young man glanced at the girl—who gave not a sign that she was even slightly aware of his existence.*

"That's more like it," said Ralph.

If anything, she paid even closer attention to her crossword puzzle. The young man watched her pencil poised over the paper, hesitating at 22: horizontal, seven letters. Twisting his head, he read the definition, "Favorite: a minion." The young man leaned close, "Darling—"

"What?" said the girl her brows arched in surprise and indignation. "What did you say?"

The young man smiled. "I said, 'Darling,'" he replied. "That's the word you're looking for. "Favorite: a minion'; the word is 'darling.'"

The girl frowned momentarily. "Oh," she said then, and smiled. "The word in the puzzle, you mean." Her white teeth flashed and her red lips curved with laughter. "For a moment," she said, "I thought you—"

The young man interrupted. "Maybe I did," he said softly. "Maybe I really meant it when I said— 'darling.'"

"Oh, murder," said Ralph. "Oh, death. If I ever tried anything like that, they'd have to thaw me out for two straight days with a blowtorch. I can see it now; she smiled, her red lips curving with laughter as she said, 'Scram, buddy, you look like a hop-head to me.' Tell me more, quick! *Then* what did *she* say?"

Fourteen blocks north of Ralph's room, at just about this same time . . .

The girl looked up now, at the young man. "Boy, what a story this is," said Louise without enthusiasm. "Now, what? *Is* our hero handsome?"

She looked at his friendly grin, and the laughter in his dark blue eyes.

"Oh, ecstasy!"

He pushed back his hat, now, in a sudden boyish gesture.

"And she saw that his toupee was slightly twisted? Nope!"

She saw the gleam, like glints on blue steel, in the tight-knit curls of his dark, shining hair.

"Oh, *tell* me," said Louise with a heart-rending sigh, "*what* bus is that? The Washington Square bus? The Twenty-third Street crosstown? I know it isn't the bus I ride every night, because I've never seen *you* there, lover. And what if I did? I do crossword puzzles on the bus, all right, but my eyes aren't queen-size."

And so Louise Huppfelt, in her two-room apartment on Fortieth Street, and Ralph Shultz, in his one-room on Twenty-sixth Street, both continued, more or less happily, reading RECIPE FOR LOVE.

"Look," said the young man, "if you don't have dinner with me, I'll haunt you till you'll just have to give in—in self-defense. So," he said softly, "make it sooner, will you? Please?" Continued on page 91.

There's an ad for soup on page ninety-one; maybe you saw it. Says: BE HAPPY! EAT SOUP FOR ENERGY— THREE TIMES A DAY! Wonder if it would work? And the people in the ad certainly look happy—Mother, Father, both children, and Grandmother all eating soup and smiling. They *look* happy, all right. Full of energy, too. Especially Grandmother. Wonder what happened to Grandfather? Probably didn't eat enough soup. Well, anyway— *(Recipe for Love. Continued.)*

"Well," said the girl, "maybe I should have dinner with you." And the young man smiled. "But then again," she said, "maybe I shouldn't." And the young man's smile collapsed. "But," she added—and his smile came back—"I will. Why don't you pick me up at my apartment around seven?"

Louise's reaction upon reading this point in the story was unfortunate. "Oh, why," she wailed, "doesn't life live up to these wonderful stories!"

Now, what do you say we skip a little? Turn to the end of the story and see how it all worked out? The young man arrived at the girl's apartment okay, and . . .

He stood there in the doorway, and for a moment he stopped breathing. A sea-green gown swept from her bare shoulders, followed every luscious curve all the way to her ankles. Her hair was alive with a light of its own, and the cream of her skin, the red of her lips, made a picture impossibly beautiful. For a mo-

*ment he actually closed his eyes, and then the miracle
spoke.*

"Why," she said, "you're dripping wet! It must be
pouring *out!*"

"Ah—yes," the young man answered, "it is. Maybe
I'd better go hunt up a cab while you wait here."

"A cab!" she answered. "Why, you'll never find
a cab in this rain. Look, we have to eat, but we don't
have to drown. You get that wet coat off and sit down
by the fireplace. I'll put on an apron and stir us up
some crepes suzette. And we'll have a quiet evening.
How does that sound?"

It didn't sound so good to Ralph Shultz, because
he threw the magazine across the room.

"How does that sound?" he said. "A quiet evening
alone with a babe like that! It sounds *wonderful,*" he
said miserably. "Marvelous! It sounds impossible! Oh,
life, *real* life, when are you *ever* going to catch up with
life in these marvelous stories?"

Well, out of the clouds, down to earth, back to
grim life. The gray, miserable, sickly daylight always
comes around, as you very well know, and you've got to
get up, go to work, work all day, and trudge home
again at night. Which is what happened to Ralph
Shultz the following day. He was coming home, walking along toward Fifth Avenue and thinking—well, it
would be nice to say he was thinking some profound
thoughts. But this is real life, don't forget, and about
all he was thinking was: What a lousy job. I'd like to
quit. I'd like to walk in and tell that old . . . Wish I
could start my own business. Raise hamsters, maybe.
They say there's money in that. Or start a diaper
service. Hire a secretary, a nice-looking one, and . . .

"Ah, *excuse* me, mister!" Ralph said aloud. "I'm
sorry! I was—"

"Hey, if de sidewalk's big enough for me, it oughta be big enough for you, Jack."

Ralph apologized to the big fat man and, resuming his thoughts, walked on. But that's enough of Ralph's thoughts. They were pretty much like the ones most of us think.

Ralph arrived at Fifth Avenue, the bus came, he got on, and—well, certainly. Of course, you've guessed it. Of *course*, Louise Huppfelt was on that bus. And you're saying, "Some coincidence, all right!" But wait a second. After all, they rode the Fifth Avenue bus every night, so once in a while they'd be *bound* to take the same one, wouldn't they? Anyway, it's only in stories that coincidences never happen. In real life they're commonplace. Happen all the time.

Well, there was Louise on the bus; not beautiful, but not bad, either. There were no mysterious high lights in her hair, but those plain ordinary high lights were pretty nice, too. And—well, what would you want Ralph to do? Sit down next to a big fat man? He sat next to Louise.

Not bad, he thought; not bad at all. Kind of cute, in fact. Wish she'd say something; ask me where some street is, maybe, or maybe drop something and I could pick it up, and . . . Hey, look—she's doing a crossword puzzle. Like the girl in that story! Hey, I wonder if I could work that same gag, and—no. Still, *maybe*. Let's see what she's working on. Twenty-nine verticle, five letters. She's got the first letter, H. Definition: "Having to do with bees."

"It's hives!" he said aloud, a little too loudly, in fact; several people turned around.

"What?" said Louise. "What did you say?"

"I said"—he spoke too quietly, now. Louise could hardly hear him—"I said—it's hives."

"Hives!" she said, her brows arched in surprise and indignation. "On *my* hands? It certainly *is not!* That's sunburn and nothing else, and I really *don't* see what business it is of yours!"

"No!" said Ralph. "No, what I mean is, that's the *word*. In the puzzle!"

"It certainly is *not*," she said coldly. "You're wrong on *every* count."

"Well, I," said Ralph. "That is, I—I only meant—I just thought—"

"Excuse me," said Louise, rising. "I get off here."

And that was that. It's too bad, of course. Too bad that life doesn't behave the way it ought to, but it seldom does. In the stories life *co-operates* with the characters in it. The word in the crossword puzzle is "darling," the conversation works out beautifully, and the girl does *not* get off the bus in the middle of it. But this girl did. She lived on Fortieth Street, this *was* Fortieth Street, so naturally she got off the bus.

"What a dope," Ralph said to himself. "What a moron you are. Did you really think it would work out like the story, you poor helpless boob? Did you think her ruby-red lips would curve with laughter, and . . . oh, nuts."

For a while he sat there, looking out the window listening to an argument between the bus driver and a poor, old, white-haired lady. Then—I know what I should have said, he thought. I should have smiled and said, very softly, "After all—what's a mere word between—friends." Then she'd have smiled, and sort of looked at me, and said, "Now, really—" Or no. No. "Friends?" she'd have said, and she'd have smile again, and I'd say, "Yes—I hope so, that is." And then she'd have said . . .

And all the way home Ralph Shultz figured out what *he* should have said, and what *she* would have

said, and—oh, he worked out some very clever remarks.
He had her laughing and giggling at some of the wonderful witty things he was saying. Only it was about
seventeen minutes too late.

Louise got to thinking, too, as she walked home
to her apartment with the cracked ceiling, on Fortieth Street. "What in the world was *wrong* with me?"
she asked herself. "Just why did I have to freeze him
dead? He wasn't really trying to act smart, poor guy.
He must have read that story about the girl on the bus.
So he was just trying to work the same gag, that's all.
Only it didn't work out quite right."

He was kind of cute, too, she thought. No magazine
illustration or anything, but—nice. She laughed.
" 'Hives,' he said. I *could* have helped him out a
little. I could have said 'Mister, the word in the story
was *darling.*' Or no. No, that might seem a little too
. . . I should have said, 'Sir, if you think I'm the kind
of girl who could *possibly* respond to the advances of
a strange man on a bus, you're absolutely right!' And
then he'd laugh, and I'd smile, and then he'd say . . ."

And by the time she got home Louise had quite a
little conversation assembled, too. But each of them
spent the evening alone. It rained that night, too. It
would have been a wonderful evening to spend by
the fireplace, just the two of them. If Louise had a
fireplace. Which she didn't.

Well, time moved on. It's been noted often that
a big city can be a lonely place, and it's true enough.
Louise went to work each day and came home again,
she ate and slept, and went to the movies pretty often.
One of them was about this young man who was
phoning his aunt and he dialed the wrong number and
called this girl by mistake and they got to talking and
they made a date and went to this amusement park and
at the shooting gallery he couldn't hit a thing and her

turn came and she was afraid of the gun so she just closed her eyes and shot and she hit the target and won this big doll. Then they rode on the roller coaster and they ate hot dogs and they ended up about three in the morning in this little diner and the man who owned it was such a nice funny old character—well, it was a pretty nice movie, and Louise felt pretty depressed afterward.

Ralph saw the same movie—just this ordinary average guy, you see, James Stewart, who meets this girl by dialing the wrong number. . . . Ralph wondered if anything like that could really happen. Just for the fun of it, next night, he tried the same thing; just closed his eyes and dialed a number, "Huffnagel Cleaning and Dyeing," said a voice, and Ralph hung up.

He took a lot of walks, too. Ralph liked to walk, he told himself, and he'd walk around for a while, maybe up Lexington Avenue, and then after a while he'd stop in at a bar. He didn't much like to drink, but he kept reading about these interesting people and conversations you run into in bars. But all anyone ever wanted to talk about was baseball.

Well, you know how it is; the one that gets away is the one you can't forget. Louise kept remembering Ralph every once in a while, and Ralph kept thinking about Louise. Days passed, a week went by, and a week or so more, but neither of them moved out of town; they didn't change their jobs or their habits, so it was only a matter of time till they got on the same bus again.

The bus was crowded and Ralph didn't see her till he stood right next to her seat. Then their eyes met, and they both looked away, very quickly. Ralph stared up at the ads and Louise went furiously to work on her puzzle. Now, in a story he'd have sat down, right next to her. But in real life he didn't. He couldn't. A big fat man was sitting there. So Ralph stared at the ads, and Louise sat there looking at her puzzle, and thinking.

Now, why cut my own throat? she thought. Like last time? Why stand on ceremony? And she began to write on her newspaper.

Ralph tried to keep looking at the ads (there was one on soup), but then he just couldn't help it; he looked down and saw that Louise was writing, very industriously, in big capital letters, in the margin of her paper. "Favorite," she wrote. "A minion."

Ralph grinned happily, leaned down and whispered. "Darling . . ."

"What?" said Louise, in a slightly tremulous voice. "What did you say?"

"I said—darling. That's the word you're looking for —isn't it?"

"Yes," she said faintly. "That's the word—I've been waiting for."

"Hey, you two screwballs want to sit together?" said the big fat man.

"Yes!" said Ralph. "We—"

"No," said Louise, "I—we get off here."

"Yeah, that's right," said Ralph softly. "We get off here. Because I've got a date—with a gorgeous brown-haired redhead!"

"With beautiful queen-size eyes," said Louise, as the fat man moved over next to the window, looking disgusted.

Well, they arrived okay—at her luxurious apartment with a loose board in the floor and no heat after ten. Louise turned and said, "She stood there; a vision in green." Then she laughed and said, "Her old, green, year-before-last coat, with a tear in the hem, and that old, old look."

"Yeah," said Ralph, "and *he* stood there—like a big drip."

"That reminds me," said Louise. "You're dripping wet. It must be *pouring* out!"

"Huh?" said Ralph. "Oh, yeah!" he said quickly. "I'm drenched! Soaked to the skin!" He coughed. "Pneumonia. Suppose I go hunt up a—streetcar, while you wait here?"

"No," said Louise, "you just go into my huge living room and find a fireplace. I'll put on my frilly little apron and stir us up some—pancakes."

Ralph grinned at her. "At this point," he said, "I suppose I ought to think up something pretty terrific. A smash punch line. And I usually do, too. About three weeks too late."

He was right about that. He kissed Louise, and then Louise kissed him, and finally Louise said, "I'm glad you read the right magazines."

And Ralph said, "So am I—honey."

Which is *exactly* what he should have said at least three weeks before! Why, if he'd been the hero in a story, he'd have recognized the setup *immediately!* He'd *never* have muffed that opportunity. Anyone with the sense a hero is born with would have known that of *course* the five-letter word beginning with "H" and having to do with bees, just *couldn't* be anything else but "Honey."

So you see? It just goes to show you. That's the trouble with you real-life people—you're so helpless! Why, the only way Louise Huppfelt and Ralph Shultz *ever* got together was to make real life live up to life as it's lived in these wonderful stories.

Which isn't a bad idea. It's something you might try yourself sometime. Who knows? Maybe it *is* a solution to world peace.

SECOND CHANCE

I can't tell you, I know, how I got to a time and place no one else in the world even remembers. But maybe I can tell you how I felt the morning I stood in an old barn off the county road, staring down at what was to take me there.

I paid out seventy-five dollars I'd worked hard for after classes last semester—I'm a senior at Poynt College in Hylesburg, Illinois, my home town—and the middle-aged farmer took it silently, watching me shrewdly, knowing I must be out of my mind. Then I stood looking down at the smashed, rusty, rat-gnawed, dust-covered, old wreck of an automobile lying on the wood floor where it had been hauled and dumped thirty-three years before—and that now belonged to me. And if you can remember the moment, whenever it was, when you finally got something you wanted so badly you dreamed about it—then maybe I've told you how I felt staring at the dusty mass of junk that was a genuine Jordan Playboy.

You've never heard of a Jordan Playboy, if you're younger than forty, unless you're like I am; one of those people who'd rather own a 1926 Mercer convertible sedan, or a 1931 Packard touring car, or a '24 Wills Sainte Claire, or a '31 air-cooled Franklin convertible —or a Jordan Playboy—than the newest, two-toned, '57 model made; I was actually half sick with excitement.

And the excitement lasted; it took me four months to restore that car, and that's fast. I went to classes till school ended for the summer, then I worked, clerking at J. C. Penney's; and I had dates, saw an occasional movie, ate and slept. But all I really did—all that counted—was work on that car; from six to eight every morning, for half an hour at lunchtime, and from the moment I got home, most nights, till I stumbled to bed, worn out.

My folks live in the big old house my dad was born in; there's a barn off at the back of the lot, and I've got a chain hoist in there, a workbench, and a full set of mechanic's tools. I built hot rods there for three years, one after another; those charcoal-black mongrels with the rear ends up in the air. But I'm through with hot rods; I'll leave those to the high-school set. I'm twenty years old now, and I've been living for the day when I could soak loose the body bolts with liniment, hoist the body aside, and start restoring my own classic. That's what they're called; those certain models of certain cars of certain years which have something that's lasted, something today's cars don't have for us, and something worth bringing back.

But you don't restore a classic by throwing in a new motor, hammering out the dents, replacing missing parts with anything handy, and painting it chartreuse. "Restore" means what it says, or ought to. My Jordan had been struck by a train, the man who sold it to me said—just grazed, but that was enough to flip it over, tumbling it across a field, and the thing was a wreck; the people in it were killed. So the right rear wheel and the spare were hopeless wads of wire spokes and twisted rims, and the body was caved in, with the metal actually split in places. The motor was a mess, though the block was sound. The upholstery was rat-gnawed, and almost gone. All the nickel plating was rusted and flaking off. And exterior parts were gone; nothing but screw holes to show they'd been there. But three of the

wheels were intact, or almost, and none of the body
was missing.

What you do is write letters, advertise in the magazines people like me read, ask around, prowl garages,
junk heaps and barns, and you trade, and you bargain,
and one way or another get together the parts you need.
I traded a Winton name plate and hub caps, plus a
Saxon hood, to a man in Wichita, Kansas, for two Playboy wheels, and they arrived crated in a wooden box—
rusty, and some of the spokes bent and loose, but I
could fix that. I bought my Jordan running-board mats
and spare-wheel mount from a man in New Jersey. I
bought two valve pushrods, and had the rest precision-
made precisely like the others. And—well, I restored
that car, that's all.

The body shell, every dent and bump gone, every
tear welded and burnished down, I painted a deep
green, precisely matching what was left of the old paint
before I sanded it off. Door handles, wind-shield rim,
and every other nickel-plated part, were restored, re-
nickeled, and replaced. I wrote eleven letters to leather
supply houses all over the country, enclosing sample
swatches of the cracked old upholstery, before I found
a place that could match it. Then I paid a hundred
and twelve dollars to have my Playboy reupholstered,
supplying old photographs to show just how it should
be done. And at eight ten one Saturday evening in
July, I finally finished; my last missing part, a Jordan
radiator cap, for which I'd traded a Duesenberg floor
mat, had come from the nickel plater's that afternoon.
Just for the fun of it, I put the old plates back on then;
Illinois license 11,206, for 1923. And even the original
ignition key, in its old leather case—oiled and worked
supple again—was back where I'd found it, and now I
switched it on, advanced the throttle and spark, got
out with the crank, and started it up. And thirty-three

years after it had bounced, rolled and crashed off a grade crossing, that Jordan Playboy was alive again.

I had a date, and knew I ought to get dressed; I was wearing stained dungarees and my dad's navy blue, high-necked old sweater. I didn't have any money with me; you lose it out of your pockets, working on a car. I was even out of cigarettes. But I couldn't wait, I had to drive that car, and I just washed up at the old sink in the barn, then started down the cinder driveway in that beautiful car, feeling wonderful. It wouldn't matter how I was dressed anyway, driving around in the Playboy tonight.

My mother waved at me tolerantly from a living-room window, and called out to be careful, and I nodded; then I was out in the street, cruising along, and I wish you could have seen me—seen *it*, I mean. I don't care whether you've ever given a thought to the wonderful old cars or not, you'd have seen why it was worth all I'd done. Draw yourself a mental picture of a simple, straight-lined, two-seater, open automobile with four big wire wheels fully exposed, and its spare on the back in plain sight; don't put in a line that doesn't belong there, and have a purpose. Make the two doors absolutely square; what other shape should a door be? Make the hood perfectly rounded, louvered at the sides because the motor needs that ventilation. But don't add a single unnecessary curve, jiggle, squiggle, or porthole to that car—and picture the radiator, nothing concealing it and pretending it doesn't exist. And now see that Playboy as I did cruising along, the late sun slanting down through the big old trees along the street, glancing off the bright nickel so that it hurt your eyes, the green of the body glowing like a jewel. It was beautiful, I tell you it was beautiful, and you'd think everyone would see that.

But they didn't. On Main Street, I stopped at a

light, and a guy slid up beside me in a great big, shining, new '57 car half as long as a football field. He sat there, the top of the door up to his shoulders, his eyes almost level with the bottom of his windshield, looking as much in proportion to his car as a two-year-old in his father's overcoat; he sat there in a car with a pattern of chrome copied directly from an Oriental rug, and with a trunk sticking out past his back wheels you could have landed a helicoptor on; he sat there for a moment, then turned, looked out, and smiled at *my* car!

And when I turned to look at him, eyes cold, he had the nerve to smile at *me,* as though I were supposed to nod and grin and agree that any car not made day before yesterday was an automatic side-splitting riot. I just looked away, and when the light changed, he thought he'd show me just how sick his big four-thousand-dollar job could make my pitiful old antique look. The light clicked, and his foot was on the gas, his automatic transmission taking hold, and he'd already started to grin. But I started when he did, feeding the gas in firm and gentle, and we held even till I shot into second faster than any automatic transmission yet invented can do it, and I drew right past him, and when I looked back it was me who was grinning. But still, at the next light, every pedestrian crossing in front of my car treated me to a tolerant understanding smile, and when the light changed, I swung off Main.

That was one thing that happened; the second was that my date wouldn't go out with me. I guess I shouldn't blame her. First she saw how I was dressed, which didn't help me with her. Then I showed her the Jordan at the curb, and she nodded, not even slightly interested, and said it was very nice; which didn't help her with me. And then—well, she's a good-looking girl, Naomi Weygand, and while she didn't exactly put it in these words, she let me know she meant to be seen tonight, preferably on a dance floor, and not waste her youth and beauty riding around in some old antique. And when I told her I was going out in the Jordan tonight, and if she wanted to come along, fine, and if she didn't—well, she didn't. And eight seconds later she was opening her front door again, while I scorched rubber pulling away from the curb.

I felt the way you would have by then, and I wanted to get out of town and alone somewhere, and I shoved it into second, gunning the car, heading for the old Cressville road. It used to be the only road to Cressville, a two-lane paved highway just barely wide enough for cars to pass. But there's been a new highway for fifteen years; four lanes, and straight as a ruler except for two long curves you can do ninety on, and you can make the seven miles to Cressville in five minutes or less.

But it's a dozen winding miles on the old road, and half a mile of it, near Cressville, was flooded out once, and the concrete is broken and full of gaps; you have to drive it in low. So nobody uses the old road nowadays, except for four or five farm families who live along it.

When I swung onto the old road—there are a lot of big old trees all along it—I began to feel better. And I just ambled along, no faster than thirty, maybe, clear up to the broken stretch before I turned back toward Hylesburg, and it was wonderful. I'm not a sports-car man myself, but they've got something when they talk about getting close to the road and into the outdoors again—the way driving used to be before people shut themselves behind great sheets of glass and metal, and began rushing along super-highways, their eyes on the white line. I had the windshield folded down flat against the hood, and the summer air streamed over my face and through my hair, and I could see the road just beside and under me flowing past so close I could have touched it. The air was alive with the heavy fragrances of summer darkness, and the rich nostalgic sounds of summer insects, and I wasn't even thinking, but just living and enjoying it.

One of the old Playboy advertisements, famous in their day, calls the Jordan "this brawny, graceful thing," and says, "It revels along with the wandering wind and roars like a Caproni biplane. It's a car for a man's man—that's certain. Or for a girl who loves the out of doors." Rich prose for these days, I guess; we're afraid of rich prose now, and laugh in defense. But I'll take it over a stern sales talk on safety belts.

Anyway, I liked just drifting along the old road, a part of the summer outdoors and evening, and the living country around me; and I was no more thinking than a collie dog with his nose thrust out of a car, his eyes half closed against the air stream, enjoying the feeling human beings so often forget, of simply being a living creature. " 'I left my love in Avalon,' " I was bawling out at the top of my lungs, hardly knowing when I'd started, " 'and saaailed awaaay!' " Then I was singing "Alice Blue Gown," very softly and gently. I sang, "Just a Japanese Saaandman!" and "Whispering," and "Barney Google," the fields and trees and cattle, and sometimes an occasional car, flowing past in the darkness, and I was having a wonderful time.

The name "Dempsey" drifted into my head, I don't know why—just a vagrant thought floating lazily up into my consciousness. Now, I saw Jack Dempsey once; six years ago when I was fourteen, my dad, my mother, and I took a vacation trip to New York. We saw the Empire State Building, Rockefeller Center, took a ride on the subway, and all the rest of it. And we had dinner at Jack Dempsey's restaurant on Broadway, and he was there, and spoke to us, and my dad talked to him for a minute about his fights. So I saw him; a nice-looking middle-aged man, very big and broad. But the picture that drifted up into my mind now, driving along the old Cressville road, wasn't that Jack Dempsey. It was the face of a young man not a lot older than I was, black-haired, black-bearded, fierce and scowling. Dempsey, I thought, that snarling young face rising up clear and vivid in my mind, and the thought completed itself: He beat Tom Gibbons last night.

Last night; Dempsey beat Gibbons *last night*—and it was true. I mean it *felt* true somehow, as though the thought were in the very air around me, like the old songs I'd found myself singing, and suddenly several things I'd been half aware of clicked together in my mind. I'd been dreamily and unthinkingly realizing that there were more cars on the road than I'd have expected, flowing past me in the darkness. Maybe some of the farm families along here were having some sort of Saturday-night get-together, I thought. But then I knew it wasn't true.

Picture a car's headlights coming toward you; they're two sharp beams slicing ahead into the darkness, an intense blue-white in color, their edges as defined as a ruler's. But these headlights—two more sets of them were approaching me now—were different. They were entirely orange in color, the red-orange of the hot filaments that produced them; and they were hardly even beams, but just twin circles of wide, diffused orange light, and they wavered in intensity, illuminating the road only dimly.

The nearer lights were almost upon me, and I half rose from my seat, leaning forward over the hood of the Jordan, staring at the car as it passed me. It was a Moon; a cream-colored nineteen-twenty-two Moon roadster.

The next car, those two orange circles of wavering

light swelling, approached, then passed, as I stared and turned to look after it. It looked something like mine; wire wheels, but with the spare on a side mount, and with step plates instead of running boards. I knew what it was; a Haynes Speedster, and the man at the wheel wore a cloth cap, and the girl beside him wore a large pink hat, coming well down over her head, and with a wide brim all around it.

I sat moving along, a hand on the wheel, in a kind of stunned ecstatic trance. For now, the Saturday-night traffic at its peak, there they all came one after another, all the glorious old cars; a Saxon Six black-bodied touring car with wood-spoke wheels, and the women in that car wore chin-length veils from the edges of their flowered hats; there passed a gray-bodied black-topped Wills Sainte Claire with orange disc wheels, and the six kids in it were singing "Who's Sorry Now?"; then I saw another Moon, a light blue open four-seater, its cut-out open, and the kid at the wheel had black hair slicked back in a varnished pompadour, and just glancing at him, you could see he was on his way to a date; now there came an Elcar, two Model T Fords just behind it; then a hundred yards back, a red Buick roadster with natural-wood spoke wheels; I saw a Velie, and a roadster that was either a Noma or a Kissel, I couldn't be sure; and there was a high-topped blue Dodge sedan with cut flowers in little glass vases by the rear doors; there was a car I didn't know at all; then a brand-new Stanley Steamer, and just behind it, a wonderful low-slung 1921 Pierce-Arrow, and I knew what had happened, and where I was.

I've read some of the stuff about Time with a capital T, and I don't say I understand it too well. But I know Einstein or somebody compares Time to a winding river, and says we exist as though in a boat, drifting along between high banks. All we can see is the present, immediately around us. We can't see the future just beyond the next curve, or the past in the many bends in back of us. But it's all there just the same. There—countless bends back, in infinite distance —lies the past, as real as the moment around us.

Well, I'll join Einstein and the others with a notion of my own; just a feeling, actually, hardly even a thought. I wonder if we aren't barred from the past by a thousand invisible chains. You can't drive into the past in a 1957 Buick because there are no 1957 Buicks in 1923; so how could you be there in one? You can't drive into 1923 in a Jordan Playboy, along a four-lane superhighway; there are no superhighways in 1923. You couldn't even, I'm certain, drive with a pack of modern filter-tip cigarettes in your pocket—into a night when no such thing existed. Or with so much as a coin bearing a modern date, or wearing a charcoal-gray and pink shirt on your back. All those things, small and large, are chains keeping you out of a time when they could not exist.

But my car and I—the way I felt about it, anyway— were almost *rejected* that night, by the time I lived in. And so there in my Jordan, just as it was the year it was new, with nothing about me from another time, the old '23 tags on my car, and moving along a highway whose very oil spots belonged to that year—well, I think that for a few moments, all the chains hanging slack, we were free on the surface of Time. And that, moving along that old highway through the summer evening, we simply *drifted*—into the time my Jordan belonged in.

That's the best I can do, anyway; it's all that occurs to me. And—well, I wish I could offer you proof. I wish I could tell you that when I drove into Hylesburg again, onto Main Street, that I saw a newspaper headline saying, PRESIDENT HARDING STRICKEN, or something

like that. Or that I heard people discussing Babe
Ruth's new home-run record, or saw a bunch of cops
raiding a speak-easy.

But I saw or heard nothing of the sort, nothing
much different from the way it always has been. The
street was quiet and nearly empty, as it is once the
stores shut down for the weekend. I saw only two
people at first; just a couple walking along far down
the street. As for the buildings, they've been there,
most of them, since the Civil War, or before—Hylesburg's an old town—and in the semidarkness left by
the street lamps, they looked the same as always, and
the street was paved with brick as it has been since
World War I.

No, all I saw driving along Main Street were—just
little things. I saw a shoe store, its awning still over
the walk, and that awning was striped; broad red and
white stripes, and the edges were scalloped. You just
don't see awnings like that, outside of old photographs,
but there it was, and I pulled over to the curb, staring
across the walk at the window. But all I can tell you
is that there were no open-toed shoes among the
women's, and the heels looked a little high to me, and
a little different in design, somehow. The men's shoes
—well, the toes seemed a little more pointed than you
usually see now, and there were no suede shoes at all.
But the kids' shoes looked the same as always.

I drove on, and passed a little candy and stationery
shop, and on the door was a sign that said, *Drink
Coca-Cola,* and in some way I can't describe the letters
looked different. Not much, but—you've seen old
familiar trademarks that have gradually changed, kept
up to date through the years, in a gradual evolution.
All I can say is that this old familiar sign looked a
little different, a little old-fashioned, but I can't really
say how.

There were a couple of all-night restaurants open, as I drove along, one of them The New China, the other Gill's, but they've both been in Hylesburg for years. There were a couple of people in each of them, but I never even thought of going in. It seemed to me I was here on sufferance, or by accident; that I'd just drifted into this time, and had no right to actually intrude on it. Both restaurant signs were lighted, the letters formed by electric-light bulbs, unfrosted so that you could see the filaments glowing, and the bulbs ended in sharp glass spikes. There wasn't a neon sign, lighted or unlighted, the entire length of the street.

On West Main I came to the Orpheum, and though the box office and marquee were dark, there were a few lights still on, and a dozen or so cars parked for half a block on each side of it. I parked mine directly across the street beside a wood telephone pole. Brick pavement is bumpy, and when I shut off the motor, and reached for the hand brake—I don't know whether this is important or not, but I'd better tell it—the Jordan rolled ahead half a foot as its right front wheel settled into a shallow depression in the pavement. For just a second or so, it rocked a little in a tiny series of rapidly decreasing arcs, then stopped, its wheels settled snugly into the depression as though it had found exactly the spot it had been looking for—like a dog turning around several times before it lies down in precisely the right place.

Crossing over to the Orph, I saw the big posters in the shallow glass showcases on each side of the entrance. *Fri., Sat. and Sun.,* one said, and it showed a man with a long thin face, wearing a monocle, and his eyes were narrowed, staring at a woman with long hair who looked sort of frightened. GEORGE ARLISS, said the poster, in "The Green Goddess."

Coming Attraction, said the other poster, *Mon.,*

Tues. and Wed. "Ashes of Vengeance," starring NORMA TALMADGE and CONWAY TEARLE, with WALLACE BEERY. I've never heard of any of them, except Wallace Beery. In the little open lobby, I looked at the still pictures in wall cases at each side of the box office; small, glossy, black and white scenes from the two movies, and finally recognized Wallace Beery, a thin, handsome, young man. I've never seen that kind of display before, and didn't know it was done.

But that's about all I can tell you; nothing big or dramatic, and nothing significant, like hearing someone say, "Mark my words, that boy Lindbergh will fly the Atlantic yet." All I saw was a little, shut-down, eleven-o'clock Main Street.

The parked cars, though, were a Dort; a high, straight-lined Buick sedan with wood wheels; three Model T's; a blue Hupmobile touring car with blue and yellow disc wheels; a Winton; a four-cylinder Chevrolet roadster; a Stutz; a spoke-wheeled Cadillac sedan. Not a single car had been made later than the year 1923. And this is the strange thing; they looked *right* to me. They looked as though that were the way automobiles were supposed to look, nothing odd, funny, or old-fashioned about them. From somewhere in my mind, I know I could have brought up a mental picture of a glossy, two-toned, chromium-striped car with power steering. But it would have taken a real effort, and—I can't really explain this, I know—it was as though modern cars didn't really exist; not yet. *These* were today's cars, parked all around me, and I knew it.

I walked on, just strolling down Main Street, glancing at an occasional store window, enjoying the incredible wonder of being where I was. Then, half a block or so behind me, I heard a sudden little babble of voices, and I looked back and the movie was letting out. A little crowd of people was flowing slowly out onto the walk to stand, some of them, talking for a moment; while others crossed the street, or walked on. Motors began starting, the parked cars pulling out from the curb, and I heard a girl laugh.

I walked on three or four steps maybe, and then I heard a sound, utterly familiar and unmistakable, and stopped dead in my tracks. My Jordan's motor had caught, roaring up as someone advanced the spark and throttle, and dying to its chunky, revving-and-ticking-over idle. Swinging around on the walk, I saw a figure, a young man's, vague and shadowy down the street, hop into the front seat, and then—the cut-out open— my Jordan shot ahead, tires squealing, down the street toward me.

I was frozen; I just stood there stupidly, staring at my car shooting toward me, my brain not working; then I came to life. It's funny; I was more worried about my car, about the way it was treated, than about the fact that it was being stolen. And I ran out into the street, directly into its path, my arms waving, and I yelled, "Hey! Take it easy!" The brakes slammed on, the Jordan skidding on the bricks, the rear end sliding sideways a little, and it slowed almost to a stop, then swerved around me, picking up speed again, and as I turned, following it with my eyes, I caught a glimpse of a girl's face staring at me, and a man my age at the wheel beside her, laughing, his teeth flashing white, and then they were past, and he yelled back, "You betcha! Take it easy; I always do!" For a moment I just stood staring after them, watching the single red taillight shrinking into the distance; then I turned, and walked back toward the curb. A little part of the movie crowd was passing, and I heard a woman's voice murmur some question; then a man's voice, gruff and half angry, replied, "Yeah, of *course* it was Vince, driving like a fool as usual."

There was nothing I could do. I couldn't report a car theft to the police, trying to explain who I was, and where they could reach me. I hung around for a while, the street deserted once more, hoping they'd bring back my car. But they didn't, and finally I left, and just walked the streets for the rest of the night.

I kept well away from Prairie Avenue. If I was where I knew I was, my grandmother, still alive, was asleep in the big front bedroom of our house, and the thirteen-year-old in my room was the boy who would become my father. I didn't belong there now, and I kept away, up in the north end of town. It looked about as always; Hylesburg, as I've said, is old, and most of the new construction has been on the out-skirts. Once in a while I passed a vacant lot where I knew there no longer was one; and when I passed the Dorsets' house where I played as a kid with Ray Dor-set, it was only half built now, the wood of the frame-work looking fresh and new in the dark.

Once I passed a party, the windows all lighted, and they were having a time, noisy and happy, and with a lot of laughing and shrieks from the women. I stopped for a minute, across the street, watching; and I saw figures passing the lighted windows, and one of them was a girl with her hair slicked close to her head, curving down onto her cheeks in sort of J-shaped hooks. There was a phonograph going, and the music—it was "China Boy"—sounded sort of distant, the orchestra-tion tinny, and . . . different, I can't explain how. Once it slowed down, the tones deepening, and someone yelled, and then I heard the pitch rising higher again as it picked up speed, and knew someone was winding the phonograph. Then I walked on.

At daylight, the sky whitening in the east, the leaves

of the big old trees around me beginning to stir, I was on Cherry Street. I heard a door open across the street, and saw a man in overalls walk down his steps, cut silently across the lawn, and open the garage doors beside his house. He walked in, I heard the motor start, and a cream and green '56 Oldsmobile backed out—and I turned around then, and walked on toward Prairie Avenue and home, and was in bed a couple hours before my folks woke up Sunday morning.

I didn't tell anyone my Jordan was gone; there was no way to explain it. Ed Smiley, and a couple other guys, asked me about it, and I said I was working on it in my garage. My folks didn't ask; they were long since used to my working on a car for weeks, then discovering I'd sold or traded it for something else to work on.

But I wanted—I simply had to have—another Playboy, and it took a long time to find one. I heard of one in Davenport, and borrowed Jim Clark's Hudson, and drove over, but it wasn't a Playboy, just a Jordan, and in miserable shape anyway.

It was a girl who found me a Playboy; after school started up in September. She was in my Economics IV class, a sophomore I learned, though I didn't remember seeing her around before. She wasn't actually a girl you'd turn and look at again, and remember, I suppose; she wasn't actually pretty, I guess you'd have to say. But after I'd talked to her a few times, and had a Coke date once, when I ran into her downtown—then she was pretty. And I got to liking her; quite a lot. It's like this; I'm a guy who's going to want to get married pretty early. I've been dating girls since I was sixteen, and it's fun, and exciting, and I like it fine. But I've just about had my share of that, and I'd been looking at girls in a different way lately; a lot more interested in what they were like than in just how good-looking they were. And I knew pretty soon that this was a girl

I could fall in love with, and marry, and be happy with. I won't be fooling around with old cars all my life; it's just a hobby, and I know it, and I wouldn't expect a girl to get all interested in exactly how the motor of an old Marmon works. But I would expect her to take some interest in how I feel about old cars. And she did—Helen McCauley, her name is. She really did; she understood what I was talking about, and it wasn't faked either, I could tell.

So one night—we were going to the dance at the Roof Garden, and I'd called for her a little early, and we were sitting out on her lawn in deck chairs killing time—I told her how I wanted one certain kind of old car, and why it had to be just that car. And when I mentioned its name, she sat up, and said, "Why, good heavens, I've heard about the Playboy from Dad all my life; we've got one out in the barn; it's a beat-up old mess, though. Dad!" she called, turning to look up at the porch where her folks were sitting. "Here's a man you've been looking for!"

Well, I'll cut it short. Her dad came down, and when he heard what it was all about, Helen and I never did get to the dance. We were out in that barn, the old tarpaulin pulled off his Jordan, and we were looking at it, touching it, sitting in it, talking about it, and quoting Playboy ads to each other for the next three hours.

It wasn't in bad shape at all. The upholstery was gone; only wads of horsehair and strips of brittle old leather left. The body was dented, but not torn. A few parts, including one headlight and part of the windshield mounting, were gone, and the motor was a long way from running, but nothing serious. And all the wheels were there, and in good shape, though they needed renickeling.

Mr. McCauley gave me the car; wouldn't take a

nickel for it. He'd owned that Jordan when he was young, had had it ever since, and loved it; he'd always meant, he said, to get it in running order again sometime, but knew he never would now. And once he understood what I meant about restoring a classic, he said that to see it and drive it again as it once was, was all the payment he wanted.

I don't know just when I guessed, or why; but the feeling had been growing on me. Partly, I suppose, it was the color; the faded-out remains of the deep green this old car had once been. And partly it was something else, I don't know just what. But suddenly—standing in that old barn with Helen, and her mother and dad—suddenly I knew, and I glanced around the barn, and found them; the old plates nailed up on a wall, 1923 through 1931. And when I walked over to look at them, I found what I knew I would find; 1923 Illinois tag 11,206.

"Your old Jordan plates?" I said, and when he nodded, I said as casually as I could, "What's your first name, Mr. McCauley?"

I suppose he thought I was crazy, but he said, "Vincent. Why?"

"Just wondered. I was picturing you driving around when the Jordan was new; it's a fast car, and it must have been a temptation to open it up."

"Oh, yeah." He laughed. "I did that, all right; those were wild times."

"Racing trains; all that sort of thing, I suppose?"

"That's right," he said, and Helen's mother glanced at me curiously. "That was one of the things to do in those days. We almost got it one night, too; scared me to death. Remember?" he said to his wife.

"I certainly do."

"What happened?" I said.

"Oh"—he shrugged—"I was racing a train, out west

of town one night; where the road parallels the Q tracks. I passed it, heading for the crossroad—you know where it is—that cuts over the tracks. We got there, my arms started to move, to swing the wheel and shoot over the tracks in front of that engine—when I knew I couldn't make it." He shook his head. "Two three seconds more; if we'd gotten there just two seconds earlier, I'd have risked it, I'm certain, and we'd have been killed, I know. But we were just those couple seconds too late, and I swung that wheel straight again, and shot on down the road beside that train, and when I took my foot off the gas, and the engine rushed past us, the fireman was leaning out of the cab shaking his fist, and shouting something, I couldn't hear what, but it wasn't complimentary." He grinned.

"Did anything delay you that night," I said softly, "just long enough to keep you from getting killed?" I was actually holding my breath, waiting for his answer.

But he only shook his head. "I don't know," he said without interest. "I can't remember." And his wife said, "I don't even remember where we'd been."

I don't believe—I really don't—that my Jordan Playboy is anything more than metal, glass, rubber and paint formed into a machine. It isn't alive; it can't think or feel; it's only a car. But I think it's an especial tragedy when a young couple's lives are cut off for no other reason than the sheer exuberance nature put into them. And I can't stop myself from feeling, true or not true, that when that old Jordan was restored—returned to precisely the way it had been just before young Vince McCauley and his girl had raced a train in it back in 1923—when it had been given a second chance, it went back to the time and place, back to the same evening in 1923, that would give them a second chance, too. And so again, there on that warm July evening, actually there in the year 1923, they got into that Jordan, standing just where they'd parked it, to drive on and race that train. But trivial events can affect important ones following them—how often we've all said: If only this or that had happened, everything would have turned out so differently. And this time it did, for now something was changed. This time on that 1923 July evening, someone dashed in front of their car, delaying them only two or three seconds. But Vince McCauley, then, driving on to race along beside those tracks, changed his mind about trying to cross them; and lived to marry the girl beside him. And to have a daughter.

I haven't asked Helen to marry me, but she knows I will; after I've graduated, and got a job, I expect. And she knows that I know she'll say yes. We'll be married, and have children, and I'm sure we'll be driving a modern hard-top car like everyone else, with safety catches on the doors so the kids won't fall out. But one thing for sure—just as her folks did thirty-two years before—we'll leave on our honeymoon in the Jordan Playboy.

CONTENTS OF THE
DEAD MAN'S POCKET

At the little living-room desk Tom Benecke rolled two sheets of flimsy and a heavier top sheet, carbon paper sandwiched between them, into his portable. *Inter-office Memo,* the top sheet was headed, and he typed tomorrow's date just below this; then he glanced at a creased yellow sheet, covered with his own handwriting, beside the typewriter. "Hot in here," he muttered to himself. Then, from the short hallway at his back, he heard the muffled clang of wire coat hangers in the bedroom closet, and at this reminder of what his wife was doing he thought: Hot, hell—guilty conscience.

He got up, shoving his hands into the back pockets of his gray wash slacks, stepped to the living-room window beside the desk and stood breathing on the glass, watching the expanding circlet of mist, staring down through the autumn night at Lexington Avenue, eleven stories below. He was a tall, lean, dark-haired young man in a pullover sweater, who looked as though he had played not football, probably, but basketball in college. Now he placed the heels of his hands against the top edge of the lower window frame and shoved upward. But as usual the window didn't budge, and he had had to lower his hands and then shoot them hard upward to jolt the window open a few inches. He dusted his hands, muttering.

But still he didn't begin his work. He crossed the room to the hallway entrance and, leaning against the doorjamb, hands shoved into his back pockets again, he called, "Clare?" When his wife answered, he said, "Sure you don't mind going alone?"

"No." Her voice was muffled, and he knew her head and shoulders were in the bedroom closet. Then the tap of her high heels sounded on the wood floor and she appeared at the end of the little hallway, wearing a slip, both hands raised to one ear, clipping on an earring. She smiled at him—a slender, very pretty girl with light brown, almost blonde, hair—her prettiness emphasized by the pleasant nature that showed in her face. "It's just that I hate you to miss this movie; you wanted to see it too."

"Yeah, I know." He ran his fingers through his hair. "Got to get this done though."

She nodded, accepting this. Then, glancing at the

desk across the living room, she said, "You work too much, though, Tom—and too hard."

He smiled. "You won't mind though, will you, when the money comes rolling in and I'm known as the Boy Wizard of Wholesale Groceries?"

"I guess not." She smiled and turned back toward the bedroom.

At his desk again, Tom lighted a cigarette; then a few moments later as Clare appeared, dressed and ready to leave, he set it on the rim of the ash tray. "Just after seven," she said. "I can make the beginning of the first feature."

He walked to the front-door closet to help her on with her coat. He kissed her then and, for an instant, holding her close, smelling the perfume she had used, he was tempted to go with her; it was not actually true that he had to work tonight, though he very much wanted to. This was his own project, unannounced as yet in his office, and it could be postponed. But then they won't see it till Monday, he thought once again, and if I give it to the boss tomorrow he might read it over the weekend . . . "Have a good time," he said aloud. He gave his wife a little swat and opened the door for her, feeling the air from the building hallway, smelling faintly of floor wax, stream past his face.

He watched her walk down the hall, flicked a hand in response as she waved, and then he started to close the door, but it resisted for a moment. As the door opening narrowed, the current of warm air from the hallway, channeled through this smaller opening now, suddenly rushed past him with accelerated force. Behind him he heard the slap of the window curtains against the wall and the sound of paper fluttering from his desk, and he had to push to close the door.

Turning, he saw a sheet of white paper drifting to

the floor in a series of arcs, and another sheet, yellow, moving toward the window, caught in the dying current flowing through the narrow opening. As he watched, the paper struck the bottom edge of the window and hung there for an instant, plastered against the glass and wood. Then as the moving air stilled completely the curtains swinging back from the wall to hang free again, he saw the yellow sheet drop to the window ledge and slide over out of sight.

He ran across the room, grasped the bottom edge of the window and tugged, staring through the glass. He saw the yellow sheet, dimly now in the darkness outside, lying on the ornamental ledge a yard below the window. Even as he watched, it was moving, scraping slowly along the ledge, pushed by the breeze that pressed steadily against the building wall. He heaved on the window with all his strength and it shot open with a bang, the window weight rattling in the casing. But the paper was past his reach and, leaning out into the night, he watched it scud steadily along the ledge to the south, half plastered against the building wall. Above the muffled sound of the street traffic far below, he could hear the dry scrape of its movement, like a leaf on the pavement.

The living room of the next apartment to the south projected a yard or more farther out toward the street than this one; because of this the Beneckes paid seven and a half dollars less rent than their neighbors. And now the yellow sheet, sliding along the stone ledge, nearly invisible in the night, was stopped by the projecting blank wall of the next apartment. It lay motionless, then, in the corner formed by the two walls—a good five yards away, pressed firmly against the ornate corner ornament of the ledge, by the breeze that moved past Tom Benecke's face.

He knelt at the window and stared at the yellow

paper for a full minute or more, waiting for it to move, to slide off the ledge and fall, hoping he could follow its course to the street, and then hurry down in the elevator and retrieve it. But it didn't move, and then he saw that the paper was caught firmly between a projection of the convoluted corner ornament and the ledge. He thought about the poker from the fireplace, then the broom, then the mop—discarding each thought as it occurred to him. There was nothing in the apartment long enough to reach that paper.

It was hard for him to understand that he actually had to abandon it—it was ridiculous—and he began to curse. Of all the papers on his desk, why did it have to be this one in particular! On four long Saturday afternoons he had stood in supermarkets counting the people who passed certain displays, and the results were scribbled on that yellow sheet. From stacks of trade publications, gone over page by page in snatched half hours at work and during evenings at home, he had copied facts, quotations and figures onto that sheet. And he had carried it with him to the Public Library on Fifth Avenue, where he'd spent a dozen lunch hours and early evenings adding more. All were needed to support and lend authority to his idea for a new grocery-store display method; without them his idea was a mere opinion. And there they all lay, in his own improvised shorthand—countless hours of work—out there on the ledge.

For many seconds he believed he was going to abandon the yellow sheet, that there was nothing else to do. The work could be duplicated. But it would take two months, and the time to present this idea, damn it, was *now*, for use in the spring displays. He struck his fist on the window ledge. Then he shrugged. Even though his plan were adopted, he told himself, it wouldn't bring him a raise in pay—not immediately, anyway, or as a direct result. It won't bring me a promotion either, he argued—not of itself.

But just the same, and he couldn't escape the thought, this and other independent projects, some already done and others planned for the future, would gradually mark him out from the score of other young men in his company. They were the way to change from a name on the payroll to a name in the minds of the company officials. They were the beginning of the long, long climb to where he was determined to be, at the very top. And he knew he was going out there in the darkness, after the yellow sheet fifteen feet beyond his reach.

By a kind of instinct, he instantly began making his intention acceptable to himself by laughing at it. The mental picture of himself sidling along the ledge outside was absurd—it was actually comical—and he smiled. He imagined himself describing it; it would make a good story at the office and, it occurred to him, would add a special interest and importance to his memorandum, which would do it no harm at all.

To simply go out and get his paper was an easy task —he could be back here with it in less than two minutes —and he knew he wasn't deceiving himself. The ledge, he saw, measuring it with his eye, was about as wide as the length of his shoe, and perfectly flat. And every fifth row of brick in the face of the building, he remembered—leaning out, he verified this—was indented half an inch, enough for the tips of his fingers, enough to maintain balance easily. It occurred to him that if this ledge and wall were only a yard above ground—as he knelt at the window staring out, this thought was the final confirmation of his intention—he could move along the ledge indefinitely.

On a sudden impulse, he got to his feet, walked to

the front closet and took out an old tweed jacket; it would be cold outside. He put it on and buttoned it as he crossed the room rapidly toward the open window. In the back of his mind he knew he'd better hurry and get this over with before he thought too much, and at the window he didn't allow himself to hesitate.

He swung a leg over the sill, then felt for and found the ledge a yard below the window with his foot. Gripping the bottom of the window frame very tightly and carefully, he slowly ducked his head under it, feeling on his face the sudden change from the warm air of the room to the chill outside. With infinite care he brought out his other leg, his mind concentrating on what he was doing. Then he slowly stood erect. Most of the putty, dried out and brittle, had dropped off the bottom edging of the window frame, he found, and the flat wooden edging provided a good gripping surface, a half inch or more deep, for the tips of his fingers.

Now, balanced easily and firmly, he stood on the ledge outside in the slight, chill breeze, eleven stories above the street, staring into his own lighted apartment, odd and different-seeming now.

First his right hand, then his left, he carefully shifted his finger-tip grip from the puttyless window edging to an indented row of bricks directly to his right. It was hard to take the first shuffling sideways step then—to make himself move—and the fear stirred in his stomach, but he did it, again by not allowing himself time to think. And now—with his chest, stomach, and the left side of his face pressed against the rough cold brick—his lighted apartment was suddenly gone, and it was much darker out here than he had thought.

Without pause he continued—right foot, left foot,

right foot, left—his shoe soles shuffling and scraping along the rough stone, never lifting from it, fingers sliding along the exposed edging of brick. He moved on the balls of his feet, heels lifted slightly; the ledge was not quite as wide as he'd expected. But leaning slightly inward toward the face of the building and pressed against it, he could feel his balance firm and secure, and moving along the ledge was quite as easy as he had thought it would be. He could hear the buttons of his jacket scraping steadily along the rough bricks and feel them catch momentarily, tugging a little, at each mortared crack. He simply did not permit himself to look down, though the compulsion to do so never left him; nor did he allow himself actually to think. Mechanically—right foot, left foot, over and again—he shuffled along crabwise, watching the projecting wall ahead loom steadily closer. . . .

Then he reached it and, at the corner—he'd decided how he was going to pick up the paper—he lifted his right foot and placed it carefully on the ledge that ran along the projecting wall at a right angle to the ledge on which his other foot rested. And now, facing the building, he stood in the corner formed by the two walls, one foot on the ledging of each, a hand on the shoulder-high indentation of each wall. His forehead was pressed directly into the corner against the cold bricks, and now he carefully lowered first one hand, then the other, perhaps a foot farther down, to the next indentation in the rows of bricks.

Very slowly, sliding his forehead down the trough of the brick corner and bending his knees, he lowered his body toward the paper lying between his outstretched feet. Again he lowered his fingerholds another foot and bent his knees still more, thigh muscles taut, his forehead sliding and bumping down the brick

V. Half squatting now, he dropped his left hand to the next indentation and then slowly reached with his right hand toward the paper between his feet.

He couldn't quite touch it, and his knees now were pressed against the wall; he could bend them no farther. But by ducking his head another inch lower, the top of his head now pressed against the bricks, he lowered his right shoulder and his fingers had the paper by a corner, pulling it loose. At the same instant he saw, between his legs and far below, Lexington Avenue stretched out for miles ahead.

He saw, in that instant, the Loew's theater sign, blocks ahead past Fiftieth Street; the miles of traffic signals, all green now; the lights of cars and street lamps; countless neon signs; and the moving black dots of people. And a violent instantaneous explosion of absolute terror roared through him. For a motionless instant he saw himself externally—bent practically double, balanced on this narrow ledge, nearly half his body projecting out above the street far below—and he began to tremble violently, panic flaring through his mind and muscles, and he felt the blood rush from the surface of his skin.

In the fractional moment before horror paralyzed him, as he stared between his legs at that terrible length of street far beneath him, a fragment of his mind raised his body in a spasmodic jerk to an upright position again, but so violently that his head scraped hard against the wall, bouncing off it, and his body swayed outward to the knife edge of balance, and he very nearly plunged backward and fell. Then he was leaning far into the corner again, squeezing and pushing into it, not only his face but his chest and stomach, his back arching; and his finger tips clung with all the pressure of his pulling arms to the shoulder-high half-inch indentation in the bricks.

He was more than trembling now; his whole body was racked with a violent shuddering beyond control, his eyes squeezed so tightly shut it was painful, though he was past awareness of that. His teeth were exposed in a frozen grimace, the strength draining like water from his knees and calves. It was extremely likely, he knew, that he would faint, slump down along the wall, his face scraping, and then drop backward, a limp weight, out into nothing. And to save his life he concentrated on holding on to consciousness, drawing deliberate deep breaths of cold air into his lungs, fighting to keep his senses aware.

Then he knew that he would not faint, but he could not stop shaking nor open his eyes. He stood where he was, breathing deeply, trying to hold back the terror of the glimpse he had had of what lay below him; and he knew he had made a mistake in not making himself stare down at the street, getting used to it and accepting it, when he had first stepped out onto the ledge.

It was impossible to walk back. He simply could not do it. He couldn't bring himself to make the slightest movement. The strength was gone from his legs; his shivering hands—numb, cold and desperately rigid—had lost all deftness; his easy ability to move and balance was gone. Within a step or two, if he tried to move, he knew that he would stumble and fall.

Seconds passed, with the chill faint wind pressing the side of his face, and he could hear the toned-down volume of the street traffic far beneath him. Again and again it slowed and then stopped, almost to silence; then presently, even this high, he would hear the click of the traffic signals and the subdued roar of the cars starting up again. During a lull in the street sounds, he called out. Then he was shouting *"Help!"* so loudly it rasped his throat. But he felt the steady pressure of the wind, moving between his face and the blank wall, snatch up his cries as he uttered them, and he knew they must sound directionless and distant. And he remembered how habitually, here in New York, he himself heard and ignored shouts in the night. If anyone heard him, there was no sign of it, and presently Tom Benecke knew he had to try moving; there was nothing else he could do.

Eyes squeezed shut, he watched scenes in his mind like scraps of motion-picture film—he could not stop them. He saw himself stumbling suddenly sideways as he crept along the ledge and saw his upper body arc outward, arms flailing. He saw a dangling shoestring caught between the ledge and the sole of his other shoe, saw a foot start to move, to be stopped with a jerk, and felt his balance leaving him. He saw himself falling with a terrible speed as his body revolved in the air, knees clutched tight to his chest, eyes squeezed shut, moaning softly.

Out of utter necessity, knowing that any of these thoughts might be reality in the very next seconds, he was slowly able to shut his mind against every thought but what he now began to do. With fear-soaked slowness, he slid his left foot an inch or two toward his own impossibly distant window. Then he slid the fingers of his shivering left hand a corresponding distance. For a moment he could not bring himself to lift his right foot from one ledge to the other; then he did it, and became aware of the harsh exhalation of air from his throat and realized that he was panting. As his right hand, then, began to slide along the brick edging, he was astonished to feel the yellow paper pressed to the bricks underneath his stiff fingers, and he uttered a terrible, abrupt bark that might have been a laugh or a moan. He opened his mouth and took the paper in his teeth, pulling it out from under his fingers.

By a kind of trick—by concentrating his entire mind

on first his left foot, then his left hand, then the other foot, then the other hand—he was able to move, almost imperceptibly, trembling steadily, very nearly without thought. But he could feel the terrible strength of the pent-up horror on just the other side of the flimsy barrier he had erected in his mind; and he knew that if it broke through he would lose this thin artificial control of his body.

During one slow step he tried keeping his eyes closed; it made him feel safer, shutting him off a little from the fearful reality of where he was. Then a sudden rush of giddiness swept over him and he had to open his eyes wide, staring sideways at the cold rough brick and angled lines of mortar, his cheek tight against the building. He kept his eyes open then, knowing that if he once let them flick outward, to stare for an instant at the lighted windows across the street, he would be past help.

He didn't know how many dozens of tiny sidling steps he had taken, his chest, belly and face pressed to the wall; but he knew the slender hold he was keeping on his mind and body was going to break. He had a sudden mental picture of his apartment on just the other side of this wall—warm, cheerful, incredibly spacious. And he saw himself striding through it, lying down on the floor on his back, arms spread wide, reveling in its unbelievable security. The impossible remoteness of this utter safety, the contrast between it and where he now stood, was more than he could bear. And the barrier broke then, and the fear of the awful height he stood on coursed through his nerves and muscles.

A fraction of his mind knew he was going to fall, and he began taking rapid blind steps with no feeling of what he was doing, sidling with a clumsy desperate swiftness, fingers scrabbling along the brick, almost hopelessly resigned to the sudden backward pull and swift motion outward and down. Then his moving left hand slid onto not brick but sheer emptiness, an impossible gap in the face of the wall, and he stumbled.

His right foot smashed into his left anklebone; he staggered sideways, began falling, and the claw of his hand cracked against glass and wood, slid down it, and his finger tips were pressed hard on the puttyless edging of his window. His right hand smacked gropingly beside it as he fell to his knees; and, under the full weight and direct downward pull of his sagging body, the open window dropped shudderingly in its frame till it closed and his wrists struck the sill and were jarred off.

For a single moment he knelt, knee bones against stone on the very edge of the ledge, body swaying and touching nowhere else, fighting for balance. Then he lost it; his shoulders plunging backward, and he flung his arms forward, his hands smashing against the window casing on either side; and—his body moving backward—his fingers clutched the narrow wood stripping of the upper pane.

For an instant he hung suspended between balance and falling, his finger tips pressed onto the quarter-inch wood strips. Then, with utmost delicacy, with a focused concentration of all his senses, he increased even further the strain on his finger tips hooked to these slim edgings of wood. Elbows slowly bending, he began to draw the full weight of his upper body forward, knowing that the instant his fingers slipped off these quarter-inch strips he'd plunge backward and be falling. Elbows imperceptibly bending, body shaking with the strain, the sweat starting from his forehead in great sudden drops, he pulled, his entire being and thought concentrated in his finger tips. Then suddenly, the strain slackened and ended, his chest touching the window sill, and he was kneeling on the ledge, his forehead pressed to the glass of the closed window.

Dropping his palms to the sill, he stared into his living room—at the red-brown davenport across the room, and a magazine he had left there; at the pictures on the walls and the gray rug; the entrance to the hallway; and at his papers, typewriter and desk, not two feet from his nose. A movement from his desk caught his eye and he saw that it was a thin curl of blue smoke; his cigarette, the ash long, was still burning in the ash tray where he'd left it—this was past all belief—only a few minutes before.

His head moved, and in faint reflection from the glass before him he saw the yellow paper clenched in his front teeth. Lifting a hand from the sill he took it from his mouth; the moistened corner parted from the paper, and he spat it out.

For a moment, in the light from the living room, he stared wonderingly at the yellow sheet in his hand and then crushed it into the side pocket of his jacket.

He couldn't open the window. It had been pulled not completely closed, but its lower edge was below the level of the outside sill; there was no room to get his fingers underneath it. Between the upper sash and the lower was a gap not wide enough—reaching up, he tried—to get his fingers into; he couldn't push it open. The upper window panel, he knew from long experience, was impossible to move, frozen tight with dried paint.

Very carefully observing his balance, the finger tips of his left hand again hooked to the narrow stripping of the window casing, he drew back his right hand, palm facing the glass, and then struck the glass with the heel of his hand.

His arm rebounded from the pane, his body tottering. He knew he didn't dare strike a harder blow.

But in the security and relief of his new position, he simply smiled; with only a sheet of glass between him and the room just before him, it was not possible that there wasn't a way past it. Eyes narrowing, he thought for a few moments about what to do. Then his eyes widened, for nothing occurred to him. But still he felt calm: the trembling, he realized, had stopped. At the back of his mind there still lay the thought that once he was again in his home, he could give release to his feelings. He actually *would* lie on the floor, rolling, clenching tufts of the rug in his hands. He would literally run across the room, free to move as he liked, jumping on the floor, testing and reveling in its absolute security, letting the relief flood through him, draining the fear from his mind and body. His yearning for this was astonishingly intense, and somehow he understood that he had better keep this feeling at bay.

He took a half dollar from his pocket and struck it against the pane, but without any hope that the glass would break and with very little disappointment when it did not. After a few moments of thought he drew his leg onto the ledge and picked loose the knot of his shoelace. He slipped off the shoe and, holding it across the instep, drew back his arm as far as he dared and struck the leather heel against the glass. The pane rattled, but he knew he'd been a long way from breaking it. His foot was cold and he slipped the shoe back on. He shouted again, experimentally, and then once more, but there was no answer.

The realization suddenly struck him that he might have to wait here till Clare came home, and for a moment the thought was funny. He could see Clare opening the front door, withdrawing her key from the lock, closing the door behind her and then glancing up to see him crouched on the other side of the window. He could see her rush across the room, face astounded and frightened, and hear himself shouting instructions: "Never mind how I got here! Just open the wind—" She couldn't open it, he remembered, she'd never been able to; she'd always had to call him. She'd have to get the building superintendent or a neighbor, and he pictured himself smiling and answering their questions as he climbed in. "I just wanted to get a breath of fresh air, so—"

He couldn't possibly wait here till Clare came home. It was the second feature she'd wanted to see, and she'd left in time to see the first. She'd be another three hours or— He glanced at his watch; Clare had been gone eight minutes. It wasn't possible, but only eight minutes ago he had kissed his wife good-by. She wasn't even at the theater yet!

It would be four hours before she could possibly be home, and he tried to picture himself kneeling out here, finger tips hooked to these narrow strippings, while first one movie, preceded by a slow listing of credits, began, developed, reached its climax and then finally ended. There'd be a newsreel next, maybe, and then an animated cartoon, and then interminable scenes from coming pictures. And then, once more, the beginning of a full-length picture—while all the time he hung out here in the night.

He might possibly get to his feet, but he was afraid to try. Already his legs were cramped, his thigh muscles tired; his knees hurt, his feet felt numb and his hands were stiff. He couldn't possibly stay out here for four hours, or anywhere near it. Long before that his legs and arms would give out; he would be forced to try changing his position often—stiffly, clumsily, his coordination and strength gone—and he would fall.

Quite realistically, he knew that he would fall; no one could stay out here on this ledge for four hours.

A dozen windows in the apartment building across the street were lighted. Looking over his shoulder, he could see the top of a man's head behind the newspaper he was reading; in another window he saw the blue-gray flicker of a television screen. No more than twenty-odd yards from his back were scores of people, and if just one of them would walk idly to his window and glance out. . . . For some moments he stared over his shoulder at the lighted rectangles, waiting. But no one appeared. The man reading his paper turned a page and then continued his reading. A figure passed another of the windows and was immediately gone.

In the inside pocket of his jacket he found a little sheaf of papers, and he pulled one out and looked at it in the light from the living room. It was an old letter, an advertisement of some sort; his name and address, in purple ink, were on a label pasted to the envelope. Gripping one end of the envelope in his teeth, he twisted it into a tight curl. From his shirt pocket he brought out a book of matches. He didn't dare let go the casing with both hands but, with the twist of paper in his teeth, he opened the matchbook with his free hand; then he bent one of the matches in two without tearing it from the folder, its red-tipped end now touching the striking surface. With his thumb, he rubbed the red tip across the striking area.

He did it again, then again, and still again, pressing harder each time, and the match suddenly flared, burning his thumb. But he kept it alight, cupping the matchbook in his hand and shielding it with his body. He held the flame to the paper in his mouth till it caught. Then he snuffed out the match flame with his thumb and forefinger, careless of the burn, and replaced the book in his pocket. Taking the paper twist in his hand, he held it flame down, watching the flame crawl up the paper, till it flared bright. Then he held it behind him over the street, moving it from side to side, watching it over his shoulder, the flame flickering and guttering in the wind.

There were three letters in his pocket and he lighted each of them, holding each till the flame touched his hand and then dropping it to the street below. At one point, watching over his shoulder while the last of the letters burned, he saw the man across the street put down his paper and stand—even seeming to glance toward Tom's window. But when he moved, it was only to walk across the room and disappear from sight.

There were a dozen coins in Tom Benecke's pocket and he dropped them, three or four at a time. But if they struck anyone, or if anyone noticed their falling, no one connected them with their source.

His arms had begun to tremble from the steady strain of clinging to this narrow perch, and he did not know what to do now and was terribly frightened. Clinging to the window stripping with one hand, he again searched his pockets. But now—he had left his wallet on his dresser when he'd changed clothes—there was nothing left but the yellow sheet. It occurred to him irrelevantly that his death on the sidewalk below would be an eternal mystery; the window closed—why, how, and from where could he have fallen? No one would be able to identify his body for a time, either— the thought was somehow unbearable and increased his fear. All they'd find in his pockets would be the yellow sheet. *Contents of the dead man's pockets,* he thought, *one sheet of paper bearing penciled notations —incomprehensible.*

He understood fully that he might actually be going to die; his arms, maintaining his balance on the ledge, were trembling steadily now. And it occurred to him then with all the force of a revelation that, if he fell, all he was ever going to have out of life he would then, abruptly, have had. Nothing, then, could ever be changed; and nothing more—no least experience or pleasure—could ever be added to his life. He wished, then, that he had not allowed his wife to go off by herself tonight—and on similar nights. He thought of all the evenings he had spent away from her, working; and he regretted them. He thought wonderingly of his fierce ambition and of the direction his life had taken; he thought of the hours he'd spent by himself, filling the yellow sheet that had brought him out here. *Contents of the dead man's pockets,* he thought with sudden fierce anger, *a wasted life.*

He was simply not going to cling here till he slipped and fell; he told himself that now. There was one last thing he could try; he had been aware of it for some moments, refusing to think about it, but now he faced it. Kneeling here on the ledge, the finger tips of one hand pressed to the narrow strip of wood, he could, he knew, draw his other hand back a yard perhaps, fist clenched tight, doing it very slowly till he sensed the outer limit of balance, then, as hard as he was able from the distance, he could drive his fist forward against the glass. If it broke, his fist smashing through, he was safe; he might cut himself badly, and probably would, but with his arm inside the room, he would be secure. But if the glass did not break, the rebound, flinging his arm back, would topple him off the ledge. He was certain of that.

He tested his plan. The fingers of his left hand clawlike on the little stripping, he drew back his other fist until his body began teetering backward. But he had no leverage now—he could feel that there would be no force to his swing—and he moved his fist slowly forward till he rocked forward on his knees again and could sense that his swing would carry its greatest force. Glancing down, however, measuring the distance from his fist to the glass, he saw it was less than two feet.

It occurred to him that he could raise his arm over his head, to bring it down against the glass. But, experimenting in slow motion, he knew it would be an awkward girl-like blow without the force of a driving punch, and not nearly enough to break the glass.

Facing the window, he had to drive a blow from the shoulder, he knew now, at a distance of less than two feet; and he did not know whether it would break through the heavy glass. It might; he could picture it happening, he could feel it in the nerves of his arm. And it might not; he could feel that too—feel his fist striking this glass and being instantaneously flung back by the unbreaking pane, feel the fingers of his other hand breaking loose, nails scraping along the casing as he fell.

He waited, arm drawn back, fist balled, but in no hurry to strike; this pause, he knew, might be an extension of his life. And to live even a few seconds longer, he felt, even out here on this ledge in the night, was infinitely better than to die a moment earlier than he had to. His arm grew tired, and he brought it down.

Then he knew that it was time to make the attempt. He could not kneel here hesitating indefinitely till he lost all courage to act, waiting till he slipped off the ledge. Again he drew back his arm, knowing this time that he would not bring it down till he struck. His elbow protruding over Lexington Avenue far below, the fingers of his other hand pressed down bloodlessly tight against the narrow stripping, he waited, feeling the sick tenseness and terrible excitement building. It grew and swelled toward the moment of action, his nerves tautening. He thought of Clare—just a wordless, yearning thought—and then drew his arm back just a bit more, fist so tight his fingers pained him, and knowing he was going to do it. Then with full power, with every last scrap of strength he could bring to bear, he shot his arm forward toward the glass, and he said, *"Clare!"*

He heard the sound, felt the blow, felt himself falling forward, and his hand closed on the living-room curtains, the shards and fragments of glass showering onto the floor. And then, kneeling there on the ledge, an arm thrust into the room up to the shoulder, he began picking away the protruding slivers and great wedges of glass from the window frame, tossing then in onto the rug. And, as he grasped the edges of the empty window frame and climbed into his home, he was grinning in triumph.

He did not lie down on the floor or run through the apartment, as he had promised himself; even in the first few moments it seemed to him natural and normal that he should be where he was. He simply turned to his desk, pulled the crumpled yellow sheet from his pocket and laid it down where it had been, smoothing it out; then he absently laid a pencil across it to weight it down. He shook his head wonderingly, and turned to walk toward the closet.

There he got out his topcoat and hat and, without waiting to put them on, opened the front door and stepped out, to go find his wife. He turned to pull the door closed and the warm air from the hall rushed through the narrow opening again. As he saw the yellow paper, the pencil flying, scooped off the desk and, unimpeded by the glassless window, sail out into the night and out of his life, Tom Benecke burst into laughter and then closed the door behind him.